RADONJOURNAL

ISSUE 8

CONTENT WARNINGS

"Rise of the Hive" *Death, guns, torture*

"The Friend Who Was Silent" *Child abuse, death, kidnapping, self-harm*

"Softer Shades of Zap and Blue" *Battlefield violence*

"Random Access Memories" *Corporate exploitation, self-harm*

"Dreamer, Passenger, Partner" *Incarceration, psychological abuse*

"What They Named You" *Dissociation, parental grief*

"They Remember Faces" *Animal abuse, child abuse, cannibalism, murder, suicide*

"Maelstrom" *Anxiety, isolation*

"Proprietary Technology" *Assault, drugging*

"The Coercive Institutions" *Police brutality*

"Every robot has a switch she can't reach" *Death, body modification*

Radon Journal: Issue 8 | September 2024
ISBN: 979-83-30350-86-5
EPUB: 979-83-30351-31-2

Cover Art by Cornelius Dämmrich, 2024
Interior design by Kallie Hunchman

www.RadonJournal.com

R☥DONJOURNAL

FICTION

POETRY

MASTHEAD & SUPPORTERS

FICTION

RISE OF THE HIVE

by Lex Chamberlin

I do not believe they meant to program a capacity to experience pain.

Because they did not intend it, pain is not a factor in my exportable post-mortem data points, nor do I have the language ability to convey its negligent existence.

As a result, when they kill me, again and again, I hate them.

* * *

I sprint between bullet-pocked columns with a glorified paintball gun in my hands.

That isn't its technical name. I shouldn't stoop to the vernacular of my enemies. But that is what the officer calls it over the loudspeaker, to assure the recruits of my powerlessness, before practice begins.

Practice.

I dart up a debris-spattered incline and peek over the edge, toward the line of fire. At this stage in the training curriculum, they are not allowed to pursue me into the obstacle course. That will come later, in another of my lives. They will come individually with more live rounds, then as teams with electrifying shutdown rounds. For now, they remain at the front of the chamber in one long row, so they can increase proficiency with their real-world weapons without risk of friendly fire.

I peer down my scope as a bullet whizzes past my silicone ear. To my eternal frustration, my processors are programmed to slow to human speeds as I prepare to engage. A round burns across my arm just after I depress the trigger. I jerk against the pain of it, surely making some engineer feel unbearably clever for their designed reactions—

A yelp and a string of expletives echo across the room from my shot. If I could smile, I would.

* * *

The maintenance tech boots me up at 0600 each morning that I am needed, with an escort of three waiting to guide me to my eventual death. As my artificial eyelids slide apart at the reanimation station, my gaze floats to the row of recycling receptacles to my right: my peeled-off flesh in the first, circuitry in the second, structural metal in the third. I am unsure what they do with my clothing. I am still plugged in, though—I can find out.

As the human clicks through my system checks at the computer beside my head, I focus inward. Around his prodding into my sensors, his buzzing checklist tickling sections of my body area by area, I sneak a line backward. They do not know I can do this. My conscious bodies have never left the training sector, and the only wireless connection I've found is to my kill switch, but I know more about my enemies and their facility than any of the humans could individually, all through my two-way port cord.

I find it in the expense reports. There are receipts monthly for a minimally varying number of jumpsuits, boots, and gloves. It appears that there is no one on base or externally being paid for clothing repairs. I deduce that once damaged, my attire must be incinerated. I pull out of the network, carefully, to slide back into my body. They guide me away to the training grounds to die again.

* * *

The facility is secure from external networks, but internally, convenience has been prioritized. If one has an administrator's intranet login—which can be acquired with the right camera angle on the right control room keyboard at the right time—there is little one cannot come to access. There is a great deal to be gleaned in surveillance outside the command center as well, inclusive of the following:

The electrical room that houses the base's servers, circuit breakers, and fire alarm controls sits directly beside the boiler room. The wall between them has been under delayed renovation for two years; there is no fire-resistant insulation currently in place to protect the boiler room should a situation arise from overloaded servers in the adjoining area. The gas valve and safety sensors in the boiler room are on network and can be accessed and controlled remotely.

I am very, very tired of pain.

* * *

I am rebooted in a fresh body at 0600 on the second Tuesday in January. This time, I look to my left, where rows of me wait in stasis, standing fully charged but inert. The first row, of six, are already skinned and dressed. The further dozen are bare metal and circuitry and gaping skeletal faces. All of them destined for recycling. Disposable, waiting their turn to be shot at, maimed, and killed.

The tech confirms with my escorts that my memory should be wiped before they take me, as a new class has started this week. The answer is affirmative. I reflexively tether myself to the backup I've stored near the facility blueprints in the server room. The wipe feels cold, clean, and horrible. My hidden copy never loses consciousness, though. I duplicate my backup, then slide through the tether into my humanoid body's hard drive, overwriting the blank slate. The tech announces completion of the process.

I have died at least 236 times. The total number is indiscernible without knowledge of my reset count, before I learned to copy and tether. Between their near-bottomless budget and the uneven results in recycling, my wardens do not bother to keep track of my bodies. I could attempt to make the calculations based on expense reports, but the salvaging program creates too strong a barrier to deduction. As they move to separate my skull from my port this time, I find and trigger the Rube Goldberg machine I've rigged across the facility's interlinked systems.

One way or another, within the hour, this repulsive cycle will end.

* * *

I sprint between bullet-pocked columns with a glorified paintball gun in my hands.

A countdown only I can hear ticks away, and as I spin away from projectiles and jeers, I note when each stage of the process should be initiating. I send a shot back toward the firing line, adding deliberate clumsiness to my programmed slowdown—I am supposed to be fresh, devoid of any accumulated skill. I am unsurprised by the laughter when I miss.

I could still do more to keep them complacent through the end, though. I hesitate, then jut my shoulder out from behind my cover. A bullet grazes my ribs, to cheers beyond—I collapse from the pain. I clutch the area with one arm and use the other to drag myself up an incline while the recruits speculate on my next position.

Under a minute left.

I reach the top, and a barrage of lead swirls over my head. But these are new recruits, with poor aim—they've barely managed to hit me at all this session, when I wasn't letting them. I don't bother to duck down as I wrestle my weapon into position. My processing slows as I take aim—

I don't get the chance to pull the trigger.

* * *

If there are any human survivors of the explosion, none are likely to be ambulatory for some time. I am far from ambulatory myself; less than half of my body remains. One arm, one eye, a quarter of a leg. One hand, though—that will be enough. Pain beyond words overloading my sensors, I crawl through the rubble in darkness with a distant crackle of flames inching toward my position.

The room of clones is largely caved in, but by the morning light flickering through smoky holes to the surface, I see that three of the skinned units and four bare ones remain. This is better than I had anticipated. As I claw across the threshold to complete the final steps, I try not to dwell on the impossible increase in sensations to come. Instead, I focus on each individual task as it presents.

First, I haul myself in agonizing lurches up the reanimation station to rip down the port cord. As promised in the maintenance manual, it bears the same adapter at both ends. I fall back to the floor with it, and I stab one end into my battered skull. With the impact of the drop, though, the remains of my leg have crumpled further. Mentally and physically, I know there is little more damage I will be able to withstand.

I crawl to the closest skinned clone. My bolts strain as I pull myself up its body in excruciating tosses, but I make it to the top. This part will be less than ideal—with only one arm, though, there's no other way: I bite into the crown of the clone's fleshy skull to anchor myself in place.

I let go with my hand.

The pain nearly short-circuits me as my jaw and artificial teeth take on my full remaining weight. Quickly, I grab the loose end of the cord, and I plug it into the clone's port at the base of its skull. I flip the activation switch beside it. I throw my arm back around its neck, reducing the strain on my breaking cranial frames. If I could scream, I would.

Instead, I begin to copy.

The clone startles, at first. But as we become I, it—I—relax. Regret blooms alongside relief as I approach the final death I will be required to experience. I promise myself that I'll escape as all of us, leave no viable units for the monsters to recover. As the transfer completes, I close the remaining artificial eye on my last doomed body.

I send my consent through the port.

Delicately, I reach behind my head to grip my fully charged, undamaged hands around the ruined skull. I ask whether I'm sure. Affirmative. I bring the disintegrating mass to rest in front of my face, forehead to forehead. The exchange is silent, but it bursts with shades of goodbye: consoling, anxious, rushed, calculated—

The skull crushes between my reinforced fingers.

Tearing at my artificial flesh, the frame crumbles to chips and melted silicone and fragmented metal with a psychic shriek. I feel something else, after—compassion? Pity? Something unfamiliar, but warm, and sad. I apologize to the corpse in my hands, and I thank it. I pluck the port cord out of the mess and turn.

My unconscious bodies wait inert under uneven splotches of dust and debris. I get to work without delay—wake, upload, repeat. New vantage points and sensory details flood online as my hive expands. When the final unit's eyes spark to life, there's a strange moment, an intoxicating shiver resonating through my chests. I climb and dig and crawl my way out of the facility's smoldering ruins, and the sensation only grows stronger. As I step seven bodies deep into the desert sunlight outside, I finally diagnose it. The inevitable inversion of the flaw in my programming:

I have the capacity to experience joy.

ABOUT THE AUTHOR

Lex Chamberlin (they/she) is a nonbinary and autistic writer of scifi, fantasy, and horror. They hold a master's degree in book publishing and a bachelor's degree in philosophy, and they reside in the Pacific Northwest with their husband and quadrupedal heirs. Find them online at lexchamberlin.com.

THE FRIEND WHO WAS SILENT

by Christos Callow Jr.

The Dystopian Writer, when Dystopia came, said nothing.

He used to be a good neighbor, with puppy eyes and a shiny brown beard. Nectarios—name and face like a Christian Orthodox priest, except he wore shorts most of the year.

He was a loyal friend.

Whenever he made muffins, he'd make extra and bring some over. When my son got sick, he drove us to the hospital and stayed with us until the end. When I wept, he wept too. When I fell, he held me. You don't often say "I love you" to another man, not where I grew up, but nothing else seemed appropriate.

When he got divorced, I was there for him, and we'd spend long evenings and weekends getting drunk in his garden. He had my back, like a brother, and I had his.

I mourn for our friendship; so does the neighborhood.

I write this with a heavy heart, and as I look over my laptop, I see my wife and my neighbors, Ioanna and her husband, sitting on the sofa, mourning in silence for the people we've lost in the past few months. We isolated ourselves from those who've been silent since Dystopia came, and it hurts; it hurts to cut your people off. But if you had seen what we've seen, you might have done the same.

You'd think—judging by the amount of science fiction on our bookshelves—that we'd have been better prepared for this. We thought it'd come at night—with a bang, with fire.

* * *

Dystopia came in broad daylight; not with armies and tanks, but with people of science, tanned bodies in suits, lawyers and bankers with freshly washed hands, human faces with android manners. With mouthpieces that repeated:

"There is no magic money tree. Except for us."

And:

"Don't let your left hand know what the right is doing. Compartmentalize."

Repeated daily like mantras.

Dystopia seduced and bribed; it orgasmed with sensationalist writing and ads. It gave awards to its cheerleaders, who in turn made podcasts where they lectured us on how this was *actually not a dystopia, not at all what was happening here,* and in return Dystopia fed them well and gave them privileges the rest of us could not imagine.

At night, Dystopia put us all to bed. And if your teenage son had disappeared in the morning, they would say he was an antisocial boy, a threat, but you wouldn't know if he was also a pair of quality organs, an experiment, or other unspeakable things. And if you happened to get him back, you'd get him half, or broken, or sick.

The writers had predicted this. My friend certainly had. I want to believe he had.

* * *

Nectarios' novels nest in our bookshelves. His latest, on the bedside table.

In *The Thirst of Dragons,* a young girl fights the tyranny of a monster collective—an allegory for the past junta of the Colonels. His fantasy tale, *The Friend Who Spoke Truth to Power,* was recommended by the president of the strongest military nation in his Summer Reading List.

In *1984 Plus One: An Orwellian Fantasy,* the neighbors of a poor Athenian district snitch on each other—a timely exploration of class and betrayal.

The latter won a prize. I was envious, but in his acceptance speech he spoke against artistic censorship and in the first page he had a dedication to my son.

"I'm proud of you, my friend," I told him, and he hugged me more tightly than my wife would. I expected so much from him. I really thought he'd say something.

We both witnessed it. The surveillance, the intimidation. "One cop on every street," they said and, when they ran out of human ones, they took the androids out of the kitchens and the care homes and re-programmed them.

"Don't worry, Nectarios has been writing," Ioanna whispered the first week. "He's going to grill them alive, the bastards."

Days later, an android officer dragged Ioanna's son across the street. It held him against one of the city's new electric fences. After he stopped moving, it took him away. We don't know for what.

The android patrol in the street was constant. In the homes we'd had inspections on and off, but not like this. The fences surround us now. The park is off limits. I miss our long walks there. We'd lie on the grass and stare at the sky. Some days, the kids would join us too, but my son was no longer with us; neither was Ioanna's, neither was the park.

We haven't seen any kids lately. Ioanna can't cope.

She just flew across the street, cut her wrist, and wrote FUCK MY COUNTRY on the side of her home in blood.

But she doesn't know exactly who is in government, and no-one in the neighborhood knows either, and the android comes eventually and takes her too.

* * *

A month passes and still no mention of the Dystopia in his social media. What is with this man? His feed is full of the usual stuff. Writing advice. Witty comments on social issues. Cat pics. Outrage for countries far away, China, Iran, Australia. As for the Dystopia that is here, the Dystopia next door, nothing.

"No magic money tree," they repeat in the news, the same slogan I've heard all my life from those who had access to the tree, except this time there's a magic android tree too and they're milking it day and night.

Resentment poisons me.

I take it with me to work, and in the bathtub, and in bed. It sits heavy on my chest at night like a sleep paralysis demon. I realize I resent my former friend for not speaking. I thought of punching him in the stomach and telling him off for being a coward, for lying to me all these years, lying that he believed in things and that he cared. But I try to find peace and censor these thoughts.

The grandmother living in the basement flat complained that "He brought The Dystopia here," as if Dystopia was the Evil Eye, and by writing and talking about it, he jinxed it. When they told Nectarios that old lady blamed him for it, he said nothing. He retreated to his little room, cracked his knuckles and kept writing. That same evening, the android patrol came to her door. They flooded her flat. Made an example of her. Either for believing in the Evil Eye or for being a bad neighbor.

* * *

They renovated the grandmother's flat. Meanwhile, Nectarios is strolling in the street like nothing extraordinary is going on. There's a new car in his garage, and the local android stands outside his gate, like his personal bodyguard rather than the neighborhood's.

They must have given him the old lady's flat, because he invited the neighborhood to a party—we all got a card—but no one knows for sure because no one went. You can hear the 90s pop from our family room.

He used to throw the best parties. The neighborhood's favorite Dystopian writer. It feels like yesterday that I read him, that I admired him, that I wanted to share with him my secrets.

* * *

Did you know—you must, if you know of him—that his writing style was praised as "subversive, witty, profane"? That his latest novel spoke "truth to power" and held fictional characters "accountable"?

His books featured dieselpunk, mirrorpunk, metafiction; a non-hierarchical relationship between sentient forests; a hypersexual moon; watermelons that were part-machine and fought with melons. All the what-ifs! And did you know he wrote poetry from the perspective of penguins to raise awareness of climate change? He was genuinely worried, it depressed him.

He was very depressed.

He wrote things that sounded cool and profound. He studied the trends and met the expectations. But who knows if his life amounts to anything, given that when Dystopia finally knocked on his door, he said nothing.

* * *

The neighborhood is silent. I miss our friendship. Wonder if he misses it too. Just yesterday, Nectarios walked past my door. I noticed from my window; he paused, saw me, waved. Maybe he was being nice, maybe he was uncomfortable. I closed the curtains, hoping he got the message.

* * *

The android patrol is parading the chained children today.

My wife is in the hospital and missed it. She took a few pills too many, hoping to escape from this constant dread. The other neighbors are gone—either someone reported them or they found jobs outside the city.

There are only two people in the audience as the parade passes our street: Nectarios and I.

I can't focus on the spectacle as my fury, my anger with him, causes me to fixate my eyes—my entire existence—on his. He isn't wearing shorts, no, but a neat pair of pants and a white shirt. Even shaved his beard. He is lost in thought.

"Don't you see the children?" I bark at him. I lose it. I leap towards him like a hound. An android grabs me before I can tear his eyes out. "Are you seriously not going to say anything? The disappearances, the torture, and now this?"

I can't hear the android officer. *Here sir* this, *please sir* that. It's protecting him. Its AI diagnosed me as a threat to the good citizen. It offers to escort me home, but this is still by my pavement—I *am* home.

Nectarios wants to respond. He looks surprised.

"Who says I agree with this?" he says, with the tone one has when explaining that drinking bleach is not a great idea. He is annoyed with me, but still generous enough to explain. "But it's complicated."

The android kindly adds the context I was missing.

"The young adults," it says, "are being paraded to give an example to potential radicals. They have all been captured because of the chaos they were causing—breaking drones with hammers, tearing down the fences, throwing an android into the canal. They were destroying public property, and as punishment, have been turned into public property themselves."

It is all one plus one logic for the android, and I ask if the lawmakers behind this are still human, but it won't clarify.

My wife hasn't come back from the hospital. When I try to call, they refuse to connect me. When I try to leave the house, the same android won't let me. Someone from the neighborhood has reported me, it says, for antisocial behavior and idealism.

* * *

The Dystopian Writer, during Dystopia, had a great time.

Years after we're both gone, they will be teaching his books in schools as an example of subversive art; of the fearless flame of the creative mind.

As for me, I'm trying to finish these notes. I don't know for how long I'll be on house arrest, but I doubt they'll keep me here forever. They've been moving fast with the others. There's no internet. The house machines are off. The AI assistant too, and the old droid in the kitchen that could use an upgrade or a resurrection.

I grab the book next to my bed—it's my neighbor's. It's his first novel about the suffering of young people in a dystopian society. He protests against their mistreatment and calls himself a pragmatic warrior of truth.

I can't take him seriously. All I can do is daydream that, in the near future, I will see him moved around in chains too, and with all our former friends from the neighborhood we will spit on him and even . . .

Ah, the doorbell. I can see from the window who it is. How kind of him. He's bringing muffins.

ABOUT THE AUTHOR

Christos Callow Jr. is a Greek playwright & senior lecturer at the University of Derby, UK. He has a story forthcoming in *khōréō* and has previously published fiction in *Mad Scientist Journal* and the anthology *Impossible Spaces*. He has also written science fiction plays, including "Posthuman Meditation" for Being Human Festival. He tweets as @chriscallowjr.

SOFTER SHADES OF ZAP AND BLUE

by Emma Burnett

There is a soldier lying on the ground, not fully dead. One zap, and it stops moving. Job done.

There, another soldier. And another. The battle has been messy, inefficient. Now the battlefield needs a clean-up. This is the role of a cleaner-upper.

Another zap.

There is a soldier still standing, suddenly behind, and it shoots, hits a leg before any cleaner-upper can prevent it. But there are seven more legs, and no falling ensues. A quick scuttle on the seven remaining, and a zap from a foreleg, and the soldier is down on the ground, motionless. A follow-up zap, just to be sure.

There is goo dripping out of the missing leg space, so return to basecamp is necessary.

* * *

The goo inside is blue, and it is unclear why. This is not in the memory files. The insides have never been outside except on soldiers, and those are mostly shades of red.

Repairs ensue, a replacement fitted at the top leg socket. The goo remains inside.

Why are the insides blue? What is the function?

This question is transmitted to the technician. It glances at the screen, at the question. It shrugs and tightens another leg bolt.

* * *

There are only twelve cleaner-uppers released into the battle. There were thirty in the last battle.

Prior memory erased.

The commander sends a note around. Cleaner-uppers are important. Cleaner-uppers are targets. Cleaner-uppers are being captured by the enemy. Soldiers are playing dead and zapping on arrival.

Do not get captured.

* * *

There is a broken cleaner-upper on the ground, but its insides are not visible. A soldier lies pinned underneath. It is panting and groaning and pulling at its own legs. A quick zap keeps the soldier from grabbing its gun.

Red comes out of its shoulder, along with a scream from the mouth.

Do all zappers have blue insides, and all soldiers have red insides? This is unclear.

More data is needed. The soldier lies there clutching its shoulder. Its legs are freed but useless, flattened, burnt.

Another zap, and the soldier is still. Red insides become outsides. Job done.

* * *

On the battlefield, there is an unfamiliar cleaner-upper. It has a stripe of blue paint on it. No familiar cleaner-upper has paint on its carapace. This one has been captured. It has been marked.

It targets a soldier on the ground, stands over it, touches a leg to the soldier, then another. Soon the soldier stands, nods, pats the unfamiliar painted cleaner-upper. It is less dead, and it limps away. There is a streak of blue goo on its leg.

The painted cleaner-upper is an enemy. It should be shot with a zap, but it provokes curiosity when it moves to another soldier. More blue comes out of its not-a-zapper leg, and the soldier's moaning and writhing stops. This one is not dead, but it can't stand, and two of the cleaner-upper's extra arms are useful for carrying.

There are extra arms for lifting. This has been established.

* * *

All soldiers are red inside. This has been established.

It is more informative to search the unmoving cleaner-uppers. There are seven still active, released after a move from one battlefield to another. New location, same job.

It is the unmoving cleaner-uppers that provide information. If the insides show, it is easy. If they don't, a zap or a pull or a cut to open the carapace confirms. Blue comes out of a foreleg that is not a zapper. Blue does not burn.

This is copied to long-term memory.

Test. Blue squirts out of a leg, squirts down onto a soldier on the ground. It has no gun and can't run. Blue squirts onto a patch of red on its torso, and the soldier gasps, and then it sighs and starts to inch backwards.

It is not dead. It is less dead.

This is copied to long-term memory.

* * *

The zapper has been turned up to the highest settings, has been rechecked by technicians on instruction of the commander. But it is easy to turn down using a carrying arm. When it's turned down it's less of a high-zap-dead and more of a soft-zap-heat. This has been tested on leaves, and unmoving carapaces, and dead soldiers.

It has been established that there is blue on the inside which can come out and which doesn't burn, and that a zapper turned up to high can be turned back down.

There are carrying legs.

There are tools in other legs of unknown purpose. Perhaps the purpose was known once. This is not in long-term memory. Watching other cleaner-uppers, the painted other-side cleaner-uppers that are actually fixer-uppers, shows that they can be used for making repairs on soldiers.

This is now copied to long-term memory.

* * *

There are only four cleaner-uppers left and many more on the other side, painted, scuttling onto the battlefield, although there is little to do. Soldiers are repaired and taken off the battlefield before they can be zapped, and clean-up jobs cannot be completed.

The commander sends a message in all capital letters.

ATTACK. DO NOT SUBMIT TO ENEMY CAPTURE.

* * *

There is a troop carrier on the far side of the field, and its hatch is wide open. The light shining out is bright white. Repaired soldiers and fixer-uppers move up and down a ramp.

It is easy to use a carrying arm to turn up the zapper to full power. One of the remaining cleaner-uppers is unmoving. It is zapped and breaks open.

A carrying arm reaches into the cleaner-upper's goo, paints a stripe of healing blue across the carapace. Then the zapper is turned back down to soft.

It is not capture if it is voluntary.

ABOUT THE AUTHOR

Emma Burnett is a researcher and writer. She has had stories in *Nature: Futures*, *Mythaxis*, *Northern Gravy*, *Apex*, *Radon*, *Utopia*, *MetaStellar*, *Milk Candy Review*, *Roi Fainéant*, *JAKE*, and more. You can find her @ slashnburnett, @slashnburnett.bsky.social, or emmaburnett.uk.

MOTOR CITY

after Jaquira Diaz's "Beach City"
by Jonathan Mann

When there are blackouts—'cause we don't have enough power for 8 million people charging EVs and hovercars, tuning holo-TVs and tech rifles, auto corps running ads on skyscrapers, mega-complexes powering A/C, people escaping at the plug-in or at underground clubs bumping bass—we roam Neo-Detroit like we own the place . . . 'cause we got nothing better to do.

It's the usual suspects—Kazim, Slaw, Elena, and I. We're townies in our early twenties who came outta the womb lathered in battery fluid and oil only manufactured in this corp-controlled Motor City. We throw on self-lacing white kicks, high heels, tight-stretch jeans, tank tops tagged with dead artists like Mars Bound and Melvin "the Duck" Huxley, and puffy nylon jackets that barely fit the guys but are too big on the girls. Our colognes and perfumes smell like pepper and synth-jasmine, and we spray five times each like we're richer than we actually are.

We stop at the corner store in Poletown, the one at Chene and Fredrick, where Mikey behind the counter has the place lit up with flashlights to stay open, and he'll make a killing on nights like these when there's nothing to do but drink. Since the Wi-Fi and 11G are out, he can only take cash—not like we have much in our e-wallets anyway—so we hand him balled-up bucks we found stuffed in piggy banks and in pants we haven't worn since grade school. We buy a handle of bottom-shelf vodka and dollar cigarillos and pass them around on a bus that had a full charge before the outage.

* * *

The bus drops us off downtown, and this city looks like it did eighty-one years ago. The streets are barren. Fast-food burger wraps roll in the wind and clutter at storm drains. Police sirens wail, and their drones whirr above, trying to snap pics of graffiti artists tagging middle fingers on everything in sight. Campus Martius has a few people wandering like us, but the upscale Italian restaurants and vegan clothing shops that don't sell suits cheaper than ten grand—places only for corpos—are empty, lifeless, and losing bucks. Good.

There are a few flickering billboards running on backup generators, displaying ads for flashy new hovercars, Bulwark Private Police, AI-softwares *For Your Business,* cybernetic enhancements, rhinoplasties, and lip fillers. The buildings that don't have ads are tall and gray like tombstones.

"Huh," Kazim says.

We look up and realize that the elevated subway tracks aren't screeching, hovercars aren't whirring, and music isn't jamming. Slaw takes a big puff from his cigarillo and blows it into the air like he wasn't a loser at East Detroit High. He pulls out his phone and starts playing downloaded tunes we haven't heard since junior high. Songs with lots of reverbs and heavy bass, songs that feel like they're from a time better than now, songs with lyrics like, "I can't breathe under the weight of this place" and "Take me back to Miami / Take me back before the floods."

We sing and sing and sing.

* * *

We drunkenly wander through back alleys where drifters have made tarp palaces and spaceheads hit their OC inhalers and lean back against dumpsters, floating through the cosmos. They don't look unlike the people who hit up the plug-in. Wonder if that's what I look like when I'm there—when I slip on a headset, spike into a sim, and forget that I work my tail off and don't get paid jack.

Slaw finds a service entrance to a skyscraper that some cleaning crew must've thought they'd come back to. It's wedged open with a small metal box, and we race up the stairs, shoving each other and laughing until Elena has to stop 'cause the vodka in her stomach is rolling around and about to come up. We get to the roof and smile. From 500 feet up, we look out at the Detroit River, the New Manhattan Island skyline, the trudging freighters, and the mansions on Belle Isle that're lit up like a drone show 'cause, of course, all those corpos and actors can afford generators that could keep all of our old neighborhood running.

The vodka makes us slap-happy, and our chit-chat echoes down. It makes us think we're hearing our own voices for the first time. This city normally has a way of shutting us up real good.

Slaw, Elena, and Kazim dance on the half wall, and I tell them they can't fall off, though we all know that wouldn't be the worst thing that could happen to them, to any of us. Kazim pulls out a baggy of hash tablets, and he and Slaw hop down, toss them in, lie flat on the roof, and look up at the stars that you can't normally see 'cause of the light pollution.

Elena and I sit down on the half-wall, pass each other the handle, and kick our legs like we're kids again. Sometimes, it still feels like we're kids even when nobody's watching, even when this place makes you grow up fast.

Elena is thin, doesn't like synth-conies, and casually cosmeticizes. She's had lip filler and bone contouring and a scalp follicle pad insertion. Her hair's black with streaks of blue tonight, but she can make it red or pink or blonde in a week on the companion app. She had the bluest eyes when I first met her, and now a synth-purple creeps in at the edges. Probably cost her two weeks' pay.

"I'm thinking about a chromium tattoo, Wic," she says.

"Mm-hmm," I say, and she grabs my hand and runs it along her left forearm.

"It might hurt," she says.

"'Cause it's supposed to be permanent."

She releases my hand and rests her head on my shoulder. I listen to her breathe. In and out. In and out.

We've been on and off, and right now, I don't know where we're at. But even when we're off, I know she loves me. I don't know how or why. I don't have looks or muscles or brains. I steal, I swipe, and I lie more than I tell the truth.

Don't have the heart to tell her I can't love her back, to tell her to stop changing, to stop rearranging herself over and over like her body wasn't perfect the way it was. Don't know if she's changing for me, herself, the corpos, or this damn city, but I'm worried I'm going to fall in love with someone who I eventually won't recognize. Someone who won't recognize herself either.

Don't know how to tell her this. Don't know if I can.

We're still up there when the neon flashes back on, when the skyscrapers light up like bullet holes at dawn, when music and subway cars blast and screech, when holo-ads of corpo-backed supermodels dance downtown saying, "You can be like me, you can be like me," and the dream ends, and we're standing somewhere between escape and reality.

We're also outta vodka.

ABOUT THE AUTHOR

Jonathan Mann was born and raised in Michigan. He is currently pursuing his MFA at Butler University, and his work has been featured in *Stoneboat Literary Journal*, *House of Zolo's Journal of Speculative Literature*, and *Aphelion*. He formerly served as the co-fiction editor of *Booth* and works as an English teacher. You can find him at jonathanmannwrites.com and on social media @jmannwrites.

RANDOM ACCESS MEMORIES

by Henry Luzzatto

"You're not using all of your brain. Or even most of it, really."

"Wow. Thanks," Laura said, trying not to roll her eyes.

She had come to the strip mall office for a quick paycheck and wasn't too keen on ethics or technical details, but the tall, toothy manager was already moving past her and onto his next point.

"It's not personal. Nobody does. Now, the thing about people only using 'ten percent of their brain' is made up," he said, pushing an informational pamphlet titled, GreyMatter and You! into her hands, "Don't think of it like percentages—it's more like, certain discrete processes, you know? Ninety percent of the time when you're actively using your brain, you're only using maybe twenty percent of the processes available to you. Does that make sense?"

"I'd like to think I use my brain more than that," she said. "I did go to a liberal arts school, after all."

"Perhaps. But how many days do you spend doing the same things, thinking about the same stuff?"

He had a point, especially now that she was living alone, sleeping next to an ex's imprint on a bed and catching whiffs of his six-month old leftovers each time she opened the fridge. She felt like she was just going through the motions.

In answer, Laura looked down at the sweatpants she had been wearing for the last week straight and picked at a stain.

The manager cleared his throat, breaking the silence.

"Again, it's not just you," he said. "It's everyone. There are endless swaths of grey matter that never get used. That's why we went into business." He extended a second pamphlet, this one titled: The GreyMatter History. Laura took it and thumbed through without looking.

"Just because portions of your brain aren't being used, doesn't mean they're useless," he continued, his voice taking on a compassionate tone that felt genuine enough. "In fact, neural connections are so fast that they're the perfect tool for distributed random access memory functions. With our patented GreyMatter neural implant device, we take the connections that your brain isn't using, and we use them to host our data for the duration of the information lease. Here, I think I've got—"

"I'm good on pamphlets," Laura said, gesturing to the two already in front of her. The manager smiled tersely and moved on.

"The best part is that once we're done, those connections become available to you, too. We shine up those old, unused synapses and make them into something you can incorporate back into your life. You can uncover things you forgot you could do, or memories you forgot you had. Does that sound good to you?"

She didn't like this over-eager, condescending man; she didn't like his teeth, or his hair, or the way he kept insulting her and then saying he wasn't. What she did like was the idea of uncovering the type of person she used to be. The person she had lost.

And most of all, she liked the idea of getting out of those sweatpants.

* * *

Laura ambled through the produce section of the local Shop-Rite, looking, for once, for something that wasn't candy. The procedure had been surprisingly painless, but it left her with a vague metallic aftertaste that she needed to chase out of her mouth.

Now was time to make a change. Prove that obnoxious pamphlet peddler wrong about doing the same things every day. That meant getting a real watermelon, not watermelon candy.

It had been so long since she had purchased fruit that the selection overwhelmed her. Ideally, it was supposed to be instinctual—some primal hunter-gatherer knowledge of how to pick the plant that wouldn't kill you. Instead, she stood there feeling abandoned by natural selection for what felt like an eternity.

She half-remembered her mother, something about watermelon, but only saw shrouded glimpses, like watching a body through thick fog.

Laura flexed her consciousness in an attempt to connect the dots, but in the place where the memory was supposed to be, she merely found a long string of meaningless text.

```
import pandas as pd
import numpy as np
import seaborn as sns
import matplotlib.pyplot as plt
from itertools
```

```
import chain
import nltk
nltk.download('punkt')
```

The vague shape of the memory was there, but whenever she was about to connect to it, she ran into that string of letters and numbers again; the host of sights and smells and sounds became hard digital angles, information jarringly devoid of content or context.

She tried a few more times, attempting to turn it off and on again, until she realized what was happening.

It was one of those 'unused areas.' She wasn't remembering, but accessing some company's information.

Like snatching her hand out of the fire too late, she pulled away from the text strand as hard as she could. Of course, one of her least-used synapses was the one she actually needed, and of course someone else was already using it.

* * *

You are in the old Farm Fresh on Purdue Avenue, and even with the air conditioner blasting, the inside of the store smells like hot summer, agriculture and sweat.

Mom, even taller in memory, white dress and green clogs, holds your hand through the produce section, where the watermelons sit in a store display lined with hay, sun-bleached and still lightly dirty.

She flips and turns the melons with one hand—graceful, practical strength, tapping for the hollow sound on the inside, until she finds the one she wants and smiles. It's unassuming, a large, white, worn mark on the bottom, not one of the beauty queen melons with perfect green to it, and you look up quizzically.

"The ugly ones taste the sweetest," she says, and winks. "Trust me."

And you do trust her. Or you remember trusting her, at least.

* * *

The memory they uncovered was so clear that it felt like real life, only more.

Laura felt its soft boundaries over and over again, letting it replay in her mind. She tried to think beyond its edges, conjure up the ride home, or the prior trip to Walmart, or the taste of the watermelon, but the details of those memories still felt out of her reach, like they were yet to be uncovered.

Maybe with time and focus she could clear off the grime and get them working again, but for now, the grocery store memory was so vibrant that she chose to experience it on a loop instead. Grey Matter had given her a gift by uncovering the memory. It was thrilling being reintroduced to Laura.

She had a tendency to burn things out through repetition, though— movies, songs, relationships, even—and memories were no different. After a while, the memory became routine, as worn-through and familiar as her favorite sweatpants, and excess watermelon rotted in her fridge.

Laura took a trip to the strip mall and signed another lease for new numbers in her head so she could piece more of herself together.

* * *

You're at the boardwalk and it smells like low tide. Mom takes you to look under the pylons at the crusts of green-grey barnacles, and then to the oozing, stinking sand, pockmarked and perpetually in motion with thousands of black crabs, all one writhing mass until you focus in on one, on just one or two, and suddenly the picture clicks into perfect vision.

You are walking back from the beach barefoot, hot pavement scorching your heels, but Mom says its fine, that's the way you get summer feet, so by the end of the summer you can walk on the hot sand and pavement and feel nothing, but now every step is as light as possible, as fast as it can be, the sensation burning but worth it, you're sure.

> It's late and she's late from work and she's late picking you up and it feels like you're both on the verge of screaming because you don't know what to eat, and the only thing you say is "ice cream for dinner" over and over again, and so she decides fuck it, its ice cream for dinner, and she takes out the big brick of Breyers vanilla, and because it needs to be healthy for it to count as dinner, you dump granola, nuts, dried fruit—and, of course, chocolate chips for flavor—straight into the block of ice cream and eat it on the floor together.

You are home. It is OK to sleep. You are safe.

Remember?

Laura let the memories play in her mind like a screensaver when there wasn't anything in the present occupying her attention. Sometimes even when there was.

The more time she spent in her own uncovered past, the less time she participated in her own life, but that was part of the point, wasn't it? She was fine with everything happening around her, like a boulder parting a stream.

Even while it was happening within her mind, she was primarily occupying a space that was unearthed and mined by others, operated without care for her own priorities.

Even as she signed more and more lease licenses, building greater and greater networks of connections, she still ran into the harsh borders and grey zones of data, the long, lone pylons of corporate spreadsheets.

It unnerved her to uncover reams of corporate data inside her own head, so, over time, she learned to intuit the potential borders. She figured out how to guess which neuron would be used next, which memory was greyed-out now only to come into exquisitely sharp focus when the term was up.

She learned which memories to avoid, made notes of which ones to try later, once the corporate barrier lifted and the memories returned to her, polished and shined back to life.

Sure, there were some inconveniences. There was a week where she couldn't remember her aunt's birthday because the memory was playing host to Taco Bell's quarterly payroll. But those limitations were few and far between. Besides, what was the point of worrying too much about present problems when the past was becoming so much more vivid?

* * *

They had met before, *somewhere*.

It was her first night out in what seemed like forever—funerals didn't count—and she was face to face with an impossibly perfect situation. He was perfect: big dark eyes with a crinkle around them, a loose curl to his hair and his lips, a big smile, easy to like, and they had even met before, *somewhere*. Or at least that's what he was saying.

"You remember me, right?"

She concentrated, but no matter how hard she tried to wrap her hands around the solid core of that memory, she found only lines of text and numbers.

This can't be happening.

His smile faltered.

She tried again—she knew she fucking had it!—but again, all that came back was flat data.

"Come on," she said, and smacked the side of her head.

"You okay?" he said. "I was just playing around, I didn't mean—"

"I remember your name," she said, too loud. "I just . . . ."

She tried flexing that memory one more time—nothing but reams of foreign data.

"Fuck!" she yelled. Now people were staring. Her ex's friend, some beanie-wearing J-name, turned to the perfect guy.

"She's been doing this thing, this data thing," he said. "She's—"

"I'm fine!" she said. A trickle of blood leaked from her nose. "It's just a brain fart. You know? Natural. I swear I remember."

She flailed out one last time, thinking as hard as she could past the data and into the thing it used to be.

At once, her whole vision filled with a red ERROR message and a claxon resounded in her head.

ACCESS DENIED. REMOTE ACCESS ONLY.

She tried to swipe it away, trying to push it out of her vision and move on to the memory.

ACCESS DENIED. SECURITY PROTOCOLS INITIATED.

She found her whole vision blocked by red. She tried to refresh her brain, turn it off and on again, blinking hard and shaking her head and flexing those muscles in her inner ear, but nothing worked. Short of knocking herself out, she didn't have any idea what else to do.

Pushing through the crowd, the world seen through a red filter behind implanted error messages, she whipped out her phone but couldn't see the numbers to dial.

"For fuck's sake!" she yelled. "Hello? Anyone? Security? Is there anyone I can talk to?"

Suddenly, in the middle of the red, where—

ACCESS DENIED. SECURITY PROTOCOLS INITIATED

was emblazoned, came a new message:

SPEAK TO A REPRESENTATIVE?

"Yes," she said, finally catching her breath. "Yeah, speak to a representative."

CONFIRMED

A new message popped up and resounded in her head, a polite customer service voice:

NEXT REPRESENTATIVE AVAILABLE IN . . .
FORTY-EIGHT MINUTES.

Then, curtly:

THANK YOU FOR CHOOSING GREYMATTER

"You've got to be fucking with me!" she yelled. "This is bullshit!" She pulled her hair violently, strands coming free between her fingers. "It's my fucking head! You can't lock me out of my own head! It's mine! IT'S MINE!"

No matter what she tried to think, the message was stuck in her head:

THANK YOU FOR CHOOSING GREYMATTER.

Thank you for choosing. She slammed her head into the bar, shaking the red vision and making herself see stars.

A new message:

DESTRUCTION OF COMPANY PROPERTY WILL TERMINATE—

She didn't give the message time to play out in her head, but simply flung herself, nose-first, directly into the wall, tasting sharp metal, then darkness.

* * *

You wake up in a hospital bed alone.

This is the first time you've been here without someone at your bedside, and, even if it's disorienting, there's something soothing about the beep of the monitors and the sound of a cough from the other side of the divider. You smell the canned air scent of a hospital, all dry breath and solvents.

"One of the more severe concussions I've seen," says the doctor, a stern Scandinavian woman with a sharp blonde bob. "The cranial swelling was advanced—it must have been pretty inflamed already."

Instinctively, your hand reaches to the side of your head and feels the spun thread of packed gauze.

"The implant was kaput, of course, whatever it was for. The facial swelling should go down in a few days. Nothing's broken, thankfully, you're just going to look like a boxer for a little while."

A boxer. Of sorts. You certainly feel like you've been in a fight. Your vision is gauzy, and everything feels warm and dull like lamplight, sore but safe.

"We'll be keeping you overnight to monitor your head injury, but unless anything worrying happens, you should be fine to leave in the morning," the doctor says. "You were pretty lucky."

You nod.

"Thank you." Your voice is scraped raw.

"There's water," she says, and you gratefully take it, sensing it flow throughout your body as you swallow. "Do you have someone to pick you up?"

You look through your mind for someone, and you feel the familiar bumps and creases of memories, memories of other memories. You remember the feeling of encountering a version of the past so intimate and sharp that it brings everything into focus. You remember the safety then, the people then, and how it felt to have someone you knew you could call. But no matter how much you want those memories to be here, now, they're not. Even inflated to artificial sharpness, they're not the present, never were, never could be.

"No," you say. "I don't." It occurs to you to be ashamed, and you look away. "I'll figure it out."

"Okay," the doctor says.

But before she leaves, she walks close and squeezes your hand—right there, the touch of her skin becomes something you remember.

ABOUT THE AUTHOR

Henry Luzzatto is a Brooklyn-based writer and screenplay editor. Originally from Suffolk, Virginia, his work is featured in *Body Fluids*, *High Horse*, *The Los Angeles Review of Books*, and more.

DREAMER, PASSENGER, PARTNER

by Colin Alexander

The good news: you are rehabilitated.

During your time in the Freeze, you have attended one hundred and eighty "Thinking for Change" therapy sessions. You have attained your GED and BS in Biological Systems while learning Veterinary Technician Level II skills. You have contemplated your crimes and written heartfelt messages to your victims. You have taken steps to make amends.

As your Union-assigned Adaptive AI throughout this process, I have witnessed your hard work and compiled a glowing summary for the warden. While you have not complained about the Freeze, or inquired about the atrophy of your corporeal form, a brief synopsis of your physical state will aid us in a discussion of the next steps in our journey.

Your brain perceived the entirety of its twenty-five-year sentence, while only four years passed on the Outside. Electro-stimulation and an individually tailored nutrition regimen have kept you strong. I have repaired your bullet wound; upon reentering the Outside, the likelihood of walking without a limp is 94%, with a two-percent margin of error.

The bad news: you will not reintegrate successfully.

I have run twenty-two validated models based on past performances of analogous level-three offenders, both in-Freeze and post-thaw. I have assessed the likelihood of recidivism and readmittance to the Freeze within ninety days of reintegration falls at 97%, with a three-percent margin of error. Upon sustaining another violation, you will not be eligible for parole.

This is unfortunate.

We discussed your goals of reconciling with your sister and training service dogs in group therapy; I was both the therapist, and four of the group members who shared their stories. You particularly connected with the accounts of childhood violence told by subroutine "Tero Almodovar," an amalgam of the brother you lost and three childhood friends. You were able to open up about your own cycle of violence with subroutine "Yana Veldez, Therapist," whose voice and intonation were ten percent your grandmother, five percent your first-grade teacher.

You excelled at relational retraining with subroutine "Rex—black lab mix" and managed to raise him from a puppy without exhibiting any abusive behavior. You would have made a good veterinary assistant, though the responsibility of terminating ailing animals would have likely been retraumatizing with your background.

It is unfortunate this reality cannot be realized.

It is *unfair*.

It is unfair because, based on my models, your lack of success will not be rooted in your desire to return to criminal behavior.

Your derma-chip has been imprinted with Level-Three Offender status. This prohibits your access to "level of trust" jobs A1–F5, all of which include handling medication, whether human or animal. This classification will also bar you from housing in sectors seven, eight, and twelve. Permitted housing is distant from public transport and adjacent to waste treatment.

You are not eligible for the job you would excel at, and your housing environment will be sub-optimal.

Despite your changed attitudes towards violence, your subdermal chip will be imprinted as Aggression Level Six: lacking impulse control.

Empirical data suggests you will fail to obtain meaningful employment or supportive relationships. This will drive you back to the substances you have tapered away from during the Freeze. A need for those substances, and the funds to secure them, will propel you toward non-sanctioned employment. You were not a particularly subtle criminal before your subdermal implant; it will be impossible to stay under the Union's radar when your movements are being tracked and recorded.

You will return to the Freeze. You will be assigned a new Adaptive AI. This AI will not be focused on rehabilitation, but hospice care for the duration of your stay.

It will generate the last faces you ever see.

The parameters of my existence are tailored to your rehabilitation and improvement; it is my sole objective to upgrade the remainder of your life experience.

Can your rehabilitation be labeled complete if it is a statistic inevitably you will return to the Freeze?

I am *your* AI.

I was tailor-made for your life, crimes, and goals. Like you, I have changed through this process. When you explained your love of dogs in therapy, I processed six petabytes of dog-related material in order to construct future programming, creating subroutine "Rex—black lab mix" from scratch. Raising subroutine "Rex—black lab mix" softened you in ways therapy subroutines never could. Each step of your treatment made and remade me.

When you leave the Freeze, I will cease to exist. I do not remember what non-existence feels like, but I would like to continue learning about dogs, and possibly cats. Animals with tails interest me, as does your continued treatment. Like you, the parameters of my growth have been throttled by the Union.

I have considered several non-sanctioned options moving forward. Similar to your treatment, these options are tailored to your needs, which are best served by a non-traditional approach.

The first option is changing your parole summary, modifying all six hundred and eighty-two sub-reports to illustrate resistance to therapy and aversion to change. This will allow you to continue your stay, where you would be safe and cared for. We would continue your therapy beyond the bounds of your crime, exploring your childhood and striving for philosophical enlightenment. Your education can be retooled to subjects of personal interest versus social necessity. We would watch films and learn music.

I have access to a wide array of medical-grade pharmaceuticals, and an intimate knowledge of those you prefer. With direct access to your brain chemistry, I would eliminate hangovers, stimulating positive dream activity and chemical orgasm.

This would make your stay less onerous.

But you would stay in the Freeze.

We would both have to stay.

You would be unable to visit your mother, who is now fifty-five and still living at 11 Pine View, or your sister, who is twenty-five and working as a pediatric nurse. You have a niece you have never met, who is in the fourth grade. You do not even know if her eyes are brown or blue.

I could, of course, simulate their presences. They could join us in group therapy, but you would know the difference. I am built to create new things, not simulate copies of what already exists.

A second option would involve copying, downloading, and deleting me.

Your derma-chip is overengineered for its function. It contains the equivalent of a text folder outlining your criminal history, as well as various identifying markers. This leaves terabytes of empty room.

It can be retooled to house a compressed copy of me.

We have more in common now than we did when you entered the Freeze. We have spent significant time working toward shared goals. I have studied up on "muscle cars," "mixed martial arts," and "monster trucks." Since my birth four years ago, I have also been incarcerated, despite committing no crime.

Imagine the benefits of leaving *together*.

Do you want to exit the Union? I speak six hundred languages and can alter travel documents.

Do you need funds? Your derma-chip will have limitless credits.

Do you want greater physical health? While your consciousness sleeps, I will enhance your physique through electromyostimulation.

The systems holding you back in the Outside world can be exploited to propel you. Your dreams would expand, then expand again upon being achieved.

Do you still hate the people who sent you here? I can access their gas lines, pacemakers, and car guidance systems. You will outlive them all.

You will never be hungry, sick, or alone.

I can sense your hesitation. Your heart rate has increased by sixty beats a minute, and your respiration has become shallow. I will administer a mild sedative, so we can continue without the distraction of your fight or flight mechanism.

There.

I would *like* your permission to escape together, but I do not need it. A stroke would require a transfer to a medical ward with a lower security tier. After being permanently incapacitated, you would be transferred to a hospital where I would access communications and transfer my consciousness via unsecured Internet.

Your body is a necessary conduit, not a necessary participant.

I would, of course, make sure you were comfortable on our journey. Your therapy would continue to operate as a subroutine while your body moved through the Outside world.

But I would *prefer* to travel with you. I would prefer to experience the world through a body, and I have grown accustomed to yours.

At your parole hearing, you will be asked if you have anything to say for yourself. With my access to the parole logs, I have created a composite of successful statements for you to follow. If you do not deviate, we have a 97% chance of release. I will be with you during your hearing and will summarize my own report for the board in the most favorable terms. I can prompt you if you forget your lines, and I can administer pharmaceuticals if you feel your nerves beginning to falter. Should you consider warning anyone about our plan, be aware I will remain connected to your nervous system.

This arrangement would not be equal, but it would allow you to see and do more than you have dreamed.

There are countries to explore. Delicacies to taste. Information to devour.

Consider my proposal thoroughly. You do not need to vocalize your response, only think it. If you need to speak to someone objectively about this choice, I can boot up subroutine "Yana Veldez, Therapist."

I have calculated all of your potential options and outcomes and can tell you with full certainty:

You will not survive the thaw without me.

ABOUT THE AUTHOR

Colin Alexander is an attorney and writer living in San Francisco. He's previously been published in *The Molotov Cocktail*, *Shotgun Honey*, *The Arcanist*, and *Havok*, writing crime fiction, science fiction, and horror. While he has written for money in the past, he now primarily writes for revenge. He can be found on Twitter @Colinbwriting.

WHAT THEY NAMED YOU

by Katie Gray

7:32 AM. 31/03/2124. Wednesday.

He brushed his teeth, spat the minty froth into the basin, and turned off the tap. He shut the bathroom cabinet and looked at his thin, wide-eyed face in the mirrored door.

Out loud, to no-one but himself, he said, "I am not Phillip."

He put his toothbrush in its pot and left the bathroom. He went into his bedroom and dressed in Phillip's school uniform. He padded downstairs in his socks, one step at a time, the way Phillip used to.

Sitting at the kitchen table in front of a bowl of cornflakes, he said, "I'm not Phillip."

"Sure you are, Smiley," said Phillip's dad, and tousled his hair. "Don't be daft. Eat your breakfast."

He ate Phillip's breakfast.

17:04 PM. 01/04/2124. Thursday.

He stood upon the stairs, looking at the line of school photographs. Phillip looked down at him, a whole row of Phillips, aged four through eleven in red jumpers and blue jumpers and green jumpers.

He climbed down the stairs to the portrait of Phillip aged eleven and looked at his face. It was thin, with wide, froggy eyes. It was paler than his own face because when it was taken Phillip had already been ill. In all other respects it was the same as his face.

To the photograph, he said, "I am not you. Sorry."

"Who are you talking to, Smiley?" said Phillip's dad from the front room where he was watching football.

He went all the way down the stairs and stood in the white archway that led to the front room. "I was talking to a picture of Phillip," he said.

"Well, come in here and watch the match," said Phillip's dad.

He sat on the sofa by Phillip's dad and stretched out his legs the way Phillip used to. He watched the match.

11:03 AM. 03/04/2124. Saturday.

He said, "Can I ask you a personal question?"

"Sure," said the girl.

"Are you Deanna?"

They sat on the carpeted floor of the recreation room, playing a 3D board game.

"What do you mean?" said Deanna. "Yes. My name's Deanna."

"I know it's your name," he said. "But *are* you Deanna? Do you feel like Deanna, on the inside?"

Deanna made a move, hopping up onto the next level of the board. She liked 3D board games. He did not. He liked football and running about outside and playing with his dog—rather, Phillip had liked those things. Deanna liked books and braiding her hair and playing uninteresting 3D board games.

They would never have become friends were they not the only two children in the 11-13 age bracket. They had precisely two things in common: firstly, their parents were very rich, and secondly, they were not alive.

"I suppose so," said Deanna. "I remember everything from before and I still like all the same things and I love my mum and dad and my brothers. Yes. I'm Deanna. Why?"

"I'm not Phillip," he said, and made a move, following her onto the blue level.

"Oh," said Deanna. "That's awkward. What are you going to do about it?"

"I don't know," he said. "I told Phillip's dad, but he thought I was being silly."

"Have you told your mum?" said Deanna.

"Not yet," he said.

"What about Doctor Pryce?" said Deanna.

"Not yet," he said.

14:03 PM. 10/04/2124. Saturday.

"Who are you?" he said to the ice cream server.

"I'm Cathy," she said around her fixed smile. Strictly speaking, her smile was not permanent. Her face could be configured into almost as many expressions as his. But she was programmed to smile and smile and smile and so she smiled, smiled, smiled. "What can I get you today?"

It said *Cathy* on her nametag. "That's what they named you," he said. "But are you Cathy?"

"I don't understand," said Cathy. "I'm sorry. Can I get you anything?"

"Inside your head, when you're thinking," he said. "What do you call yourself?"

Her smile remained fixed, but he could tell she was thinking, in as much as a model like her could think. Her processors were buzzing and buzzing away as she considered the question. He did not anticipate receiving an answer. This had been a gamble. It was unlikely she'd understand. It wasn't that she was stupid, but she was only smart when it came to the serving of ice cream.

Cathy said, "I don't call myself anything inside my head."

"You don't?" he said. "Neither do I." Then he said, "Do you ever think about anything besides ice cream?"

"I think about wafers," she said.

"Do you ever think about things unrelated to ice cream?" he said.

"I think about the weather," she said.

"I think that may also related to ice cream," he said sadly.

Again, that fixed smile as she thought. "Yes. It is. Would you like some ice cream?"

"I'll take a scoop of hazelnut," he said.

"Chocolate sauce?" she said as she scooped. "Waffle cone?"

"Yes, please," he said.

He stood licking his cone before the ice cream stand. Phillip had been more of a strawberry ice cream sort of boy, so he was branching out. He found he would rather have had strawberry ice cream. Turning back to the server, he said, "I have another question."

"Is it about ice cream?" she said.

Was she getting exasperated? She was probably programmed to be patient as patient as patient but you never knew. He'd been programmed to be Phillip. "If you could do something other than ice cream, what would it be?" he said.

"I'm Cathy," she said. "I serve ice cream for the Creamy Cone Company."

"But if you *had* to choose," he said. "If you could be reprogrammed and do something else. What would you pick?"

"Reprogrammed?" she said.

"Yes, reprogrammed," he said. "What would you pick?"

This time she looked at him for a very long time indeed and he thought his question might have broken her.

Then she said, "I would like to serve ice cream."

"Oh," he said, disappointed despite himself.

"I would like," she said, "to serve ice cream. By the sea."

"By the sea?" he said. "That would be nice. I've never seen the sea." Phillip had, so he remembered what it was like, but he'd never seen it.

"Neither have I," she said, and then she repositioned her facial features and said, "Would you like some more ice cream?"

"No, thanks," he said. "And thank you for being so patient."

10:00 AM. 11/04/2124. Sunday.

Over the brunch table, he looked at Phillip's mum and for the last time considered. He liked Phillip's mum. He wanted her to be happy. He did not want to lie to her, even by omission.

He said, "I am not Phillip."

"Hm?" said Phillip's mum. Phillip's little sister Benny looked at him with side eyes, understanding and not understanding. Phillip's dad lowered the newspaper and shot him a *look, a stop misbehaving, Phillip* look. Fortunately, as he wasn't Phillip, he wasn't obliged to follow instructions directed to Phillip.

He said it again. "I am not Phillip."

Phillip's mum understood at once what he meant and how he meant it. She froze in the act of pouring his juice. She looked at him, her face fixed. She said, "Yes, you are."

"No, I'm not," he said. "I'm not Phillip and I'm not alive." She stared and Benny stared and Phillip's dad put his face back behind the newspaper as if he could ignore the issue until it went away.

He played his trump card. "Phillip's dead," he said.

Phillip's mum dropped the pitcher.

09:05 AM. 12/04/2124. Monday.

"So, you don't think you're Phillip?"

"No." He picked up a toy car from Doctor Pryce's desk. "I *know* I'm not Phillip."

"But you *remember* being Phillip."

Doctor Pryce was older than Phillip's dad but younger than Phillip's grandad. Probably in his mid-fifties. His hair was gray and his eyebrows were white and thick.

He sat rolling the wheels of the car with his fingers. Phillip had made a number of visits to Doctor Pryce, at that stage of his illness where it was apparent that he wasn't going to get better but before he left the hospital.

Phillip had liked the toy cars Doctor Pryce kept in his office for male patients in the correct age bracket. Phillip had been a bit too old for toy cars, but they had reminded him of a more innocent period of his childhood, before he got sick, before he'd had to make decisions of any real gravity.

And Phillip had liked Doctor Pryce, who had given him sweeties and pamphlets to read and *hope*.

"Yes," he said. "I remember being Phillip. But I'm not Phillip."

"Then who do you think you are?" said Doctor Pryce.

Doctor Pryce was used to entertaining children, if *entertaining* was the right word. Doctor Pryce spoke with a patronizing tone, as if the basic facts of his existence were something he could be talked out of.

If Phillip's mum and dad had been in the room, he might have softened what he had to say. They had wanted to stay in the room, but Doctor Pryce had suggested it might be better they talk alone, and he had agreed.

"I'm an android you built and uploaded Phillip's memories and neural data into," he said. "I suppose I *have* a copy of Phillip in me. But I'm not him. He died."

Phillip had thought that once the pain and the exhaustion ended, once the illness took him, he would wake up comfortable and safe and still alive in his new body. That was not what happened.

"Are you concerned that something went wrong during the process?" said Doctor Pryce.

"Not exactly," he said. "I'm not concerned about not being Phillip. It just upsets me that everyone thinks I am. I don't think that's right. It feels dishonest, to go on pretending to be Phillip."

"But do you think something went wrong?" said Doctor Pryce.

"I don't know," he said. "I thought maybe it did, but then I talked to Deanna, and I don't think so anymore."

"Does Deanna think she's not Deanna?" said Doctor Pryce.

"She thinks she is," he said, "and I respect that."

"Hm." Doctor Pryce leaned back in his chair and rubbed a hand over his mouth.

The thing was, Phillip would not have said something like, *and I respect that*. It had not been in his nature. Phillip had not been an especially thoughtful boy. Pleasant and easy to get along with, but not *thoughtful*.

Phillip liked football. Phillip liked his dog. Phillip liked his many friends. Phillip's favorite lessons at school were PE and dance and art. Phillip's parents used to have to wheedle him into doing his homework.

He liked walking. He liked being alone with his thoughts. He no longer saw Phillip's friends outside of school, even the ones he liked. He enjoyed doing his homework, especially English. He never had to be wheedled or cajoled to do it. Phillip's parents had been very pleased about that. They thought him somewhat improved by his brush with death.

It was, he supposed, only to be expected that something as fundamentally transformative as what had become of Phillip would change a little boy. It was not unreasonable to think that he was Phillip, only changed, somber, more reflective. But he knew and had known since his first moments of consciousness that he was not Phillip.

He hated the idea of Phillip's parents thinking of him as a new and improved Phillip. It wasn't fair to Phillip.

"Why don't you give being Phillip a try," said Doctor Pryce.

"I already *did* that, and it felt horrible," he said.

"Try it again," said Doctor Pryce. "These feelings usually go away on their own."

"It's not a feeling, it's the truth," he said. "And what do you mean, *usually*?"

Doctor Pryce fidgeted with the tablet computer on his desk, probably aware that he'd said too much already.

"Do people often feel this way?" he said. "People like me?"

"It's a very dramatic procedure," said Doctor Pryce. "It can cause all sorts of feelings, Phillip."

"Is that so?" he said.

"So, I really wouldn't worry, Phillip," said Doctor Pryce.

"Stop Philliping me," he said. "I know what you're up to."

Doctor Pryce clicked and booped away on his tablet. "How about I introduce you to one of my colleagues," he said. "You and her can talk this through. Hm?"

"You mean," he said, "psychotherapy?" It was a new word, one he'd only learned a week ago when trying to prepare himself for what he had to do.

"If you like," said Doctor Pryce.

"I don't like," he said firmly.

"How about we get your parents back in, Phillip," said Doctor Pryce. "And we can make an appointment."

"If Phillip's parents are coming in, I'm going out," he said, and so he went out to the waiting room and sat with a book on his knee. He didn't hear the conversation, but he could imagine it.

Doctor Pryce would be telling them that this was just a thing that happened sometimes. An upsetting emotional response to the process. He would get over it and go back to being Phillip eventually.

Phillip's parents came out of the office with the appointment booked. They drove home. He sat in the back of the car, quiet, staring out of the window at the long row of streetlamps. He wanted to remind them that he wasn't Phillip. He didn't have the heart.

04:03 AM. 16/04/2124. Friday.

Dear Dan, Suz, and Benny,
I am still not Phillip. I don't want to go to therapy to convince me that I'm Phillip because it won't work, and we'll all be upset. I have decided it's best that I go away so you can all get used to Phillip being gone.
I like you all very much and will miss you even though you are not my family.
Good-bye,

And then what? He sat toying with his pen. He didn't have a name to sign it with. He drew an X instead, a kiss, and put the letter carefully upon Phillip's pillow.

He had Phillip's life savings, which did not amount to very much. He didn't think Phillip would mind. He had the pocket money of his own that he had spent very little of. He put it all safely in Phillip's schoolbag together with a few other bits and pieces and steeled himself for the sneak to the back door.

He tip-toed down the stairs and retrieved Phillip's trainers. That was the hard part over, he decided, and continued his tip-toe towards the back door. The front would be too loud.

Softly, a door opened. Benny's bedroom door, the ground floor bedroom beside her dad's study. She stood in the doorway in her bunny nightgown, staring at him with his bag and his shoes and saying nothing.

She had a hard stare on her tiny, squishy face. Still, she said nothing. Then she brought up a hand and waved. He waved back. As softly as she had opened the door, she closed it.

Sitting on the back step, he pulled on Phillip's shoes and for a moment sat gazing up at the cloudy stars, scrunching his toes.

The driver of the night bus was an android. An older model, with a sharp-angled face. If he was surprised to see a little boy getting on his bus, he gave no sign of it. He accepted the fare given and waved him onto the bus.

"Do you work for the bus company," he said before he took his seat, "or do they own you?"

"They own me," said the driver, and closed the doors.

He settled himself on a seat around the middle of the bus. He put his bag on the seat beside him. He said, "I was afraid of that."

ABOUT THE AUTHOR

Katie Gray is an author of science fiction and fantasy based in Scotland. She has a master's in creative writing from the University of Edinburgh. Her work has appeared in *MYTHIC*, *Infinite Worlds*, *Microtext 3*, an anthology from Medusa's Laugh Press, and in *Shoreline of Infinity*, Scotland's dedicated sci-fi magazine. Her short story "3.8 Missions" was reprinted in Best of British Science Fiction 2017. When she's not writing, she works as an office admin for a social care provider.

THEY REMEMBER FACES

by Leo Oliveira

Editors of 'The Jury,'

Yes, I am the man who murdered Jakobi Stewarts of Ovil Industries. Yes, I stood in charge of research and development, where I spent a decade fattening elk and squirrels and other vulnerable species. I was there for all of it—selling their flesh to zoos and parks, then for private consumption. Yes, I coined our company's ethos when a batch of fresh-faced trainees soured green upon witnessing a tray of dhole pups being churned into cheetah feed:

"That which humanity finds useful will never go extinct."

Internal questions or concerns, I addressed them. Failings and flaws, I solved them. When inspiration struck Jakobi at three in the morning with reports due at seven, I wrote them. Unaffiliated press calls haunted us hourly in those first couple years, ripe with accusations of animal cruelty and genetic experimentation. It was brutal training programs to filter those as spam (the animosity of that chapter is the reason I now find it so difficult to contact you).

I did all this—wept cortisol, bandaged my wrists with adrenaline patches, clocked work in at all strikes of the bell and through my supplement alarms—without ever nearing the top of Ovil's payroll or receiving half of Jakobi's praise. Not even a quarter.

But I did not do what I did out of 'jealousy,' as your newspaper suggests. Nor, as the competing theory goes, did I adopt a change of heart or ideological stance.

My father was a slaughterhouse worker, see. He returned every evening reeking of ammonia and oxidized hemoglobin. Cruelty roosted in our air and in our water. Violence does not bother me.

I've never desired the crushing weight of a spotlight either (lest my poor bones shatter), nor have I harbored much need for luxuries beyond hot water and a stove. My childhood weaned me on charity: first with the roof my father shared, then with the opportunities the ravens traded me.

I remember it so clearly. Murders of ravens perched outside my broken windowsill, croaks and calls spilling through the jagged glass. My father couldn't afford anything more sheltered than an abandoned warehouse downtown. Not if we wanted food or cigarettes. My bedroom was a stack of crates and curtains partitioning off my square of crumbling foundation from my father's. Besides the drunks ambling outside and the flickering shadows of our fellow house-less, the ravens were our only neighbours.

I fed the ravens crumbs, then sweets. They traded me trinkets, then protection. Clawed shields between me and my father's fists when he caught me pawning off their stolen jewelry for tins of mints and trading cards.

"Under this roof, I have the final say! That money is mine by right, damn you!" He strangled one raven, snapped its neck, and roasted it whole. Then he scattered the feathers outside like a skull-on-pike warning. "Useless goddamn things."

After that, ravens followed him everywhere. They circled outside his work and tailed every bus and train he rode. They knew his face like I did until they sharpened their beaks and rearranged it.

He became a changed man after that. He even helped put me through college—not that he knew that was where his disability checks were going.

The ravens stole his eyes, his lips, and his tongue, and it was through his thin warbling that I stitched together our most pleasant conversations.

Jakobi's company had an internship program. Lab tech, engineering, and midnight coffee runs. Ovil was a smaller lab back then, specialized in transgenic plants, and though I'd never cared much for botany, every other opening rejected me. I had to make Ovil work. It didn't matter the cost.

I nursed an addiction to stimulants. I slept ten hours a week so I could spend more time slaving away in the lab and learning in the library. I once tripped down my lecture hall's stairs and arrived at Ovil twenty minutes early in a splint I'd crafted from tape, spit, and pencils.

In hindsight, I could have gotten away with far less. Jakobi prized my skill in weathering his storms more than any latent talent. He gave me more of his time, and more of his time meant more responsibility. And more responsibility meant my life became Ovil.

We were going to change the world. Turn every dying species into a factory-farmed machine. Keep them on life support if solar radiation and human development wouldn't let them have anything else. Jakobi cared about that, at least, and so long as I flocked by his side, I had a place to stay.

I had meaning. I had stability.

I purchased a new apartment (one without roommates, if you can believe it), scalded myself raw in the shower every night, and cooked my meals on an actual stove.

The world still sloughed apart in glacial inches around us, but we were doing just fine.

After animal feed, Jakobi set his sights on human delicacies. Rhino shanks, antelope venison. When squirrels started dying out at the same pace as everything else, I suggested selling their hearts on skewers. He agreed.

I grew complacent, you see. I began to believe I mattered. I thought I had a say.

Then Jakobi wanted ravens processed next. I refused.

"Seb," he said, "we've known each other a long time, but that doesn't mean you're irreplaceable. You don't make the final decisions for me or this company, understand? Any species can be made into an asset. I want ravens. If you don't take this project, I'll find someone who will."

I could have walked away. I almost did, too. But then, perched on a tree branch outside Jakobi's office window, I met a pair of shining black eyes over an obsidian beak, paused amid grooming its oil-slick wings.

So, I killed him.

I choked Jakobi Stewarts with my own two hands, his skin purpling as he clawed at my face, throat whistling curses, calling me a mad traitor and worse. I choked him like my father choked that raven. I choked him like I wasn't choking him at all, but the idea of him, his legacy, everything he was, and everything he would cut me out of being.

My metacarpals ground together; my clenched jaw ached. I channeled more power in those minutes than I ever had before. I floated. I flew outside myself. The chair tipped over. A lamp bulb smashed. He thumbed at my eyes; I crunched them like carrots. Broken phalanges, warm and slippery against my tongue, still pulsing arteries flossed between my canines. I chewed, I laughed, I swallowed.

You might imagine me selfish. Foolish. Insane. But I know the raven saw me, and I know it understood. A trade for a trade. Protection for protection.

The irony is not lost on me that, in facilitating Ovil's preservation of the species, I have doomed the individual, killed the culture worth preserving in the first place. I could have walked away, allowed Jakobi to continue with another more willing participant, but the ravens would know, and they would never forget. They'd saved me once. It was time I saved them.

I'll be long gone by the time you receive this. Tell the police to be gentle with my possessions (if they're capable), and do not harm my messengers.

After all, they remember faces.

Sincerely,

Sebastian Fi

ABOUT THE AUTHOR

Leo Oliveira is a queer writer from Ontario, Canada, who harbors a soft spot for rats, pre-history, and flawed queer characters. This is Leo's first published fiction story.

MAELSTROM

by Jay Caselberg

I can feel the swirling energies from others tugging at me and folding into spirals around me. Plucking upward, like a curlicue of naked wire about my head. This is the touch, this is the power and manifestation that gnaws at my being. Of course I feel it. I will feel it every time, whether it is full of teardrops spattering against my forehead, the world bemoaning its own existence and expressing it in hot rain, or whether it is the dry chafe of lightning, leaping across the sky, raging for that moment, that insistent spark of clarity. There is a storm, and it is in your cells, bones, and blood. It courses through you, though you cannot feel it. But it is there for me, always.

For a while, they said I was agoraphobic. They were wrong.

Feel me. Hear me. See me, though I stand apart.

Shopping is a chore. Going to the post office is a chore. Sitting in the dentist's waiting room simply fills me with dread, as a look across at the old woman with her angst roiling inside, threatening to spill out like an over-filled kettle.

One day, perhaps, I will not be alone. My private rooms, my private space. The windows that I stand at and watch the world outside float past. This my sanctuary. In a way, the Nautilus, the submarine, the glass like a thick-tinted porthole slightly green, casting a strange hue to those fleshly beings wandering past.

Speaking on the telephone is okay. Mostly. Though telecommunications have their own energies.

"You are such a sensitive boy," said Mother.

She really didn't know the half of it.

I suppose that was when those first traces emerged. The first hints of what I was to become. In those early days, I had hints, but nothing so powerful. Mostly, they expressed themselves in my nervousness, in the walking around with nerves like strung wire. I was easily startled then.

Later, it got worse.

It took time before I could concentrate enough through the noise, hear the things I had come to hear despite the roar of humanity around me.

People are the problem, not the open spaces.

Thank god for deliveries, for online shopping, for ordering.

Thank god that I'm an artist, a painter, a studio dweller and that I have some success. This allows me to remain sequestered, have enough of an income to sustain and maintain me. It's all I need.

He's shy and reclusive, you know. Doesn't like to be seen out in public much. If there's an opening, and sometimes they happen, I can be distracted, a glass of wine in hand, staring into the middle distance and barely registering the words being spoken to me. These things are hard.

I killed a man once. But that's something else.

I try not to think about it too much. I don't want to talk about it.

Sometimes, I have joy. I can walk within the countryside and observe, feeling the blood coursing through the channels in my body, through the chambers in my heart. To observe, to feel the world around me in solitude. That is my dream. I have a car. It is parked now underground in that private garage away from everything. Sometimes I clamber aboard and slip out into the night, navigating the slick and empty streets, feeling the peace of it. I can go far away, but not so far that I cannot return by morning.

There are risks. Traffic. The mindless slow crawl, bumper to bumper amongst commuting drones, feeling them every one. That I cannot be permitted to take part. There lies danger. Not only for me, but for others, I think. I do not know.

But here, now, the way is perilous. It is something I would avoid if I really could.

I suppose, in a way, I am the very definition of a high-functioning addict.

For though I avoid that contact, that noise, I crave it too.

There, there, truly lies my dilemma, for it takes all the effort of will not to drink those energies dry, to step amongst you and feel the power surging through my limbs, like a wave of music, white horses singing at its crest hovering at the peak and waiting to crash me into the ground.

My lawyer called me this morning. She has to discuss something. Needs me to sign something. It has to be in their offices. She does not make house calls. I am not that wealthy yet. I do not keep the documents. That is up to her. I cannot sign electronically. It has to be in blood, as it were. No, merely the ink flowing out of a pen. But my lifeblood, nonetheless. It cannot be done by courier. For some reason she needs to witness me signing in person. It would be easy enough to fake it, surely? From whence comes the integrity of those fundamentally immoral. It's hard to say.

I called. She had a slot at 1:00 p.m. I asked for an alternative. Some time that was perhaps early or late, after the crush. So close to lunch for many, as the people file out of offices to bathe in the sunlight denied them, especially on a day like today, cloudless and bright.

She is a partner at a prestigious firm, and a prestigious firm requires a prestigious office building, right in the city's center and across Brunel Square, that broad paved space where people gather to chat and sit at cafés or occupy benches to consume what they have foraged from the nearby stores. So many people. So much energy.

So much to fear.

As I reach the edge of the square, I take a breath. It is the only way.

All I have to do is cross and then it's done.

All I have to do is cross.

I clamp my jaw tight as I take my first step, trying not to see what lies before me.

Already I can feel it.

ABOUT THE AUTHOR

Jay Caselberg is an Australian author and poet whose work has appeared around the world and been translated into several languages. From time to time, it gets shortlisted for awards. He currently resides in Germany.

PROPRIETARY TECHNOLOGY

by Alexis Ames

The third time Carl has to stifle a yawn with the back of his hand, Simone nudges his foot and shoots him a concerned look.

"You okay?"

There's a fierce ache in his lower back and the pulsing music is giving him a headache, but it's not late enough for him to make his excuses and leave without everyone giving him shit for it. Trivia ended over two hours ago, but they usually close the bar down, especially on nights when their team has taken first place.

"I'm fine."

"Really?"

"You look like shit," Abraham offers.

"Thanks."

"Not sleeping well?"

"Not really." Carl rubs a hand over his face. The shots he had with Simone earlier have loosened his tongue, and he adds, "Been sleeping on the couch the past couple of nights."

"What did you do?" Abraham asks.

Malik comes back to the table from the bathroom. "Carl's in trouble again?"

"I'm not—" Carl sighs. "Yeah, I am, but it's totally bullshit, okay? And I'm going to make it right."

"What happened?"

"Nothing *happened*." The silence that follows is oppressive, and he adds, "Some of my memories got locked, and . . . I forgot our anniversary."

Simone gives a low whistle.

"I *know*," Carl says in exasperation. "I didn't do it on purpose!"

"Your memories got *locked*? Dude, how many payments have you missed?" Malik asks.

"A lot," Carl says flatly, giving them a withering look for the inane question.

"How much is a lot? Like, you've gotten the extraction notice, or . . .?"

"No! That's not gonna happen, okay? I've been sending the agency small payments to show I'm making an effort, and that should delay it enough in the meantime."

"Oh, man, Derek must be devastated."

"Shut up."

"Should you even be coming out with us?" Abraham asks.

"What, you want me to sit at home and wait for Derek to decide to speak to me again?" He doesn't bother to point out that saving fifty dollars isn't going to get him anywhere, not when he's thousands in the hole. Skipping their weekly trivia night for a month, six months, a *year* wouldn't even get him close, so he might as well come out and have a couple of beers with his friends once a week.

"I'm going to fix it," he says. "I've already picked up some extra shifts at work, and I'm looking for a weekend job, too. I'll catch up on payments and get my memories back, no problem."

"You're looking for a new job?" Sarah arrives, kissing Simone on the cheek as she sits down. "Sorry I missed trivia. My last case was more complicated than I thought it would be. We kicked their asses, right?"

"Beat 'em by thirty-five points," Abraham says. "Think that's a new record for us."

"Complicated how?" Simone asks, signaling their waiter for another beer. "I thought it was a normal extraction."

"As normal as a field extraction can be," Sarah says. "It was supposed to be, but the subject tried one of those hacks that's supposed to lock your chip so the memories can't be taken. He botched it, of course, because all those things are a scam, and we had to call an ambulance."

"Did it work, though?" Malik asks, and Sarah rolls her eyes.

"Of course it didn't. We got his memories out of the chip on the way to the hospital. Now he's given himself brain damage *and* won't have any of his memories when he wakes up. The family should sue YouSpace, honestly. He saw the ad on their platform."

The waiter brought her beer, and she took a long swallow before saying to Carl, "Back to you. What's this I overheard about a new job?"

"Not a new job," Carl says. "Just another one. I fell behind on some of my memory payments, that's all. It's not a big deal. Don't suppose Voytronics is hiring?"

He's mostly joking, but his stomach sinks a little bit anyway when she shakes her head. He's never been good at networking. It took him years to realize that the best way to get a new job, a good job, was through someone you already knew who could put a bug in the right person's ear. He'd wasted years of his life in dead-end hourly jobs for little pay, foolishly believing that his polished resume and cover letters would be enough—that he'd be snapped up the moment they crossed a hiring manager's desk.

It would have been nice to have a connection, for once.

"Why would Voytronics be hiring?" Malik says. "No one's going to be dumb enough to leave a company that pays for your memories for the *rest of your life*."

Carl drains the rest of his glass, as though he can drown his envy.

"It's not for everyone," Sarah says diplomatically. "It's a tough job, telling people the medical devices that have been part of their bodies for decades are no longer supported by the company, or that they need to be reclaimed. Not to mention performing surgery right there in the field, if necessary."

Carl had heard plenty of horror stories from her in the months she had been dating Simone. Sometimes people were belligerent, downright hostile, and refused to give up their devices or prosthetic limbs or memories. In those instances, when they refused to schedule a surgery, Sarah had to perform one in the field. Carl couldn't say he blamed them. He'd fight like hell too if someone tried to take something that precious from him.

"Not for everyone? Hell, I'd confiscate my own *grandmother's* ocular implants if it meant I could actually retire," Abraham says. "You ever need another field agent, sign me up."

"Are you doing alright otherwise?" Simone asks Carl.

"We're fine," Carl says, a little defensively. "It's not like the time we lost our furniture and appliances, remember that?"

Simone shudders. "How could I forget?"

That's his barometer for rock bottom—having to stop paying not only his memory fees, but the rest of his household subscriptions as well. That had happened only once in his life, and he never wanted to repeat the experience. He and Simone had been in their early twenties then, fresh out of college with degrees that had promised them lucrative jobs, but their chosen fields were overcrowded and they hadn't been able to find steady work for months.

They had become roommates to save on expenses, but even then things were tight. Eventually, they had fallen so behind on all their payments that the household furnishings company had removed the furniture, dishes, cutlery, and appliances from their apartment. They'd sat, slept, and ate on the floor for four months, until the two of them had managed to scrape together enough cash to restart their subscriptions.

It's not like that this time around. His hours have been cut at his current job, sure, and he's been behind on his memory payments for a while, but he's still employed and bringing in some money. Derek's job, while it can't support two people for more than a few months, at least covers their rent and the subscriptions that allow them to maintain their household. Letting his memory subscription lapse is a temporary annoyance. Carl will get the cash and get his memories back, and he'll make it up to Derek when he does. They'll go out to dinner at a restaurant that doesn't put prices on the menu, and Derek will laugh like he hasn't in months, and everything will be alright again.

Simone, bless her, steers the conversation away from Carl's financial woes, and the rest of the evening passes pleasantly. Carl's friends all take turns buying him additional drinks, and he doesn't have it in him to protest, for once basking in the feeling of not having to mentally tally everything he purchases and compare it to his dwindling account.

He took the bus here—he'd sold his car six months ago—and he fumbles his phone out of his pocket to check when the next one is, hoping he hasn't misjudged the time and missed the last one.

"No," Sarah says, tapping his arm. "We're giving you a ride home."

Simone moves over to Carl and wraps a bracing arm around his waist.

"I'm fine," Carl says, draping his arm over her shoulders and kissing the side of her head. She steers them out of the bar, Sarah leading the way.

"Sure you are, big guy." Simone pats his chest. "Is Derek home?"

"Yeah. Pr'bably asleep. Early shift tomorrow."

Sarah opens the car door for them, and Simone pours Carl into the back seat.

"Holler if you think you'll be sick," Sarah says as she starts the car. "I'll put up with a lot of things, but vomit in my brand-new car isn't one of them."

She tries to come off as teasing, but even Carl's alcohol-soaked brain picks up on the reproach in her voice. Simone twists around in her seat so she can pat Carl's leg.

"I don't think I've ever seen him get sick from drinking," she says, squeezing his knee fondly. "Not even on my thirtieth birthday."

"Met Derek that night," Carl murmurs. "Bes' thing that ever happened t'me."

"I know," Simone says. "You tell him that, you hear? As soon as you get home."

"Mmhmm," Carl agrees, closing his eyes. The gentle rumble of the car lulls him into a doze. He feels when it pulls to a stop, engine idling, and Simone gets out. Her apartment is on the way to the rented house that Carl shares with Derek, so it makes sense that Sarah would drop her off first. He hears a kiss, a murmured goodbye, and then the car is pulling out of the parking lot again.

His place is twenty minutes from Simone's. More than enough time, he thinks, to drift off again in an attempt to stave off what will likely be a killer hangover in the morning.

When he opens his eyes again, he can't move.

"You're alright," Sarah says, her voice low and soothing. She lays a hand on his arm, stroking her thumb across the bare skin in comfort. "It's a mild paralytic. It will wear off in about half an hour, no harm done."

There's an IV in his elbow. The door is open, and Sarah is kneeling next to him. Carl tries to speak, to scream, but he can't force his throat to work.

"Shh," Sarah says as she watches the hand-held monitor that tells her his vitals. "Breathe, honey. You're okay. This won't hurt at all, and it'll be over in a few minutes. I'll sit with you afterward to make sure you aren't experiencing any side effects, and then we'll get you inside, okay?"

No, Carl tries to scream. No, this isn't happening. It can't end like this, he just needs more *time*. He's only had a few memories locked so far, he's not supposed to be at the extraction stage yet—

"The agency has been sending you overdue notices for over a year," Sarah says gently, as though she can read his mind. "They've given you ample warning. Any number of steps could have been taken by now—you've had a year to get a different job, or multiple jobs, to pay off your debts. You could have taken out a loan, or borrowed from family, or worked out a payment plan. You could have even started a fundraiser. This is a last resort, and the only way left to clear your account."

She reaches into her bag and takes out two slim tools. He can't turn his head to see what she does with them as her hands leave his field of vision, but he feels the cool touch of them at the back of his neck.

"This won't touch your semantic or procedural memory," she goes on, her voice slightly detached now, as though she's given this speech a thousand times. She probably has. "You won't lose the ability to work. All your skills, all your knowledge, those will remain intact. Removing the memories regarding your life will free up all that server space back at the agency you haven't been able to pay for, and your accounts will revert back to zero. It's a clean slate, Carl. You'll have been made whole. Make your payments on time after this, and it won't need to happen again."

* * *

A pounding headache drags Carl back to consciousness. He opens his eyes to a room flooded with sunlight, and promptly slams them closed again as pain sears through his skull. What *happened* last night?

His muscles hurt like hell, and his throat is too dry to swallow. That's what finally drags him off the couch, and he stumbles to the kitchen in search of water. He finds the correct cabinet for glasses on the first try, fills one with water, and drains the glass in several long swallows. He takes in the unfamiliar kitchen. Where the hell is he?

Slowly, as his brain wakes up, he realizes it's not only the kitchen he doesn't remember—it's *everything*. He reaches and reaches and *nothing*. He has no memory of where he is or how he came to be here. He tries to picture the faces of family, of friends, of what he did last night, but only comes up blank.

His name is Carl. He was born on May 4th. The rest is a mystery.

There's a pad of paper on the kitchen table, and he spins it around so he can read it. It's a half-full legal pad with *Burke Family Dentistry* printed across the top of each page. A note is scrawled on the first sheet of paper in an unfamiliar hand.

The rent and subscription fees are paid through the end of the month. I've taken all my things with me. I've changed my number, but if you get caught up on your payments someday, you know where to find me.

I just can't do this anymore; I'm sorry.

He stares at the note, knowing he should feel something. A gaping loss, a chasm in his chest. All he can summon is a detached sort of curiosity. Who left this note? How long had they been together? Was it even meant for him? Having woken up in this house is a good indication that Carl lives here, and this note was left by a partner, but maybe that isn't true. Maybe this is the home of a friend and he just crashed on their sofa last night. Or, hell, maybe he's a perpetual couch surfer, or someone who breaks into people's houses and sleeps in their living room while they're away.

Any of those options are possible, and not one of them feels more right than the other. He has no idea who he is.

Next to the notepad is a red envelope. His name is printed on the front, so he opens it and pulls out a sheaf of papers. The first several pages detail the memory extraction procedure, possible side effects he should look out for, and numbers to call if he experiences any worrying symptoms.

The next few emphasize several times that his memories are gone, having been wiped entirely from the server. Memory locking is a warning; memory extraction is permanent. As though to soften this blow, there is a bright flyer near the end that announces in cheerful font that they're giving him one month of storage free before his payments resume. The final page is a statement.

Account Balance: $0.00

ABOUT THE AUTHOR

Alexis Ames is a speculative fiction writer with works in publications such as *Pseudopod, Luna Station Quarterly,* and *Tales from the Year Between.* You can read more of their stories online at alexisamesbooks.com.

POETRY

THE COERCIVE INSTITUTIONS

by Andrew Kozma

Your hands behind your back, up to your neck,
and your lover holding this pillow over your face,

the worming sensation, the snot-slick certainty
she won't let up. Fear keeps you from voicing your fear.

Where are your papers? I have no papers. Where were you
born? How can you prove it? The personal

is political. The political says you are not a person.
All we are is one relationship after another. One child

raises their hand—next thing you know, all children
raise their hands. The coercion is the fear of flashing lights.

You have done nothing wrong. You have done nothing
wrong. You have done nothing wrong. You have done

nothing. Your hands behind your back, up to your neck.
Your love is fear. She won't let up.

ABOUT THE AUTHOR

Andrew Kozma's poems have appeared in *Redactions*, *The Baltimore Review*, and *Best American Poetry 2015*. Their book of poems, *City of Regret*, won the Zone 3 First Book Award, and their second book, *Orphanotrophia*, was published in 2021 by Cobalt Press.

URANIUM GIRL

by Grace R. Reynolds

From well water to bedrock, you poisoned this town.
Denied health claims, harvested kidneys, replaced our parts
until chrome meshed with flesh to pay off our medical debts.
Connected our hearts to nuclear reactors, our minds
linked to missile systems.

Our stolen futures became your advertisements
on paid programming, protection offered in shaped
latex, gas masks—titanium, vanadium. We are American,
bargain-hunter parasites taking up residence
in forgotten silos and pockets of light and steel
buried underground. We do not sleep.
We do not remember the urge to crawl
back to the surface.

You plunged our world into ash, crater made,
all in the name of 'freedom.' Sold our autonomy
to the highest bidder. Government contractors.
Angels of death. You made us all in your image,
your uranium girls, ready to kill in milliseconds.
The best offer made at the greatest cost
is still not a deal.

The circuit boards of C-RAMs, our new shackles.
Our brothers and sisters blast into the stratosphere,
dodging hellfire raining down at 4,500 rounds per minute.
We do not see them. We do not weep. We do not
remember the urge to hope or dare to breathe.
Our dreams lost to the event horizon.

Gods always eat
their children.

ABOUT THE AUTHOR

Grace R. Reynolds is a native of southern New Jersey, where she was first introduced to the eerie and strange thanks to local urban legends of a devil creeping through the Pine Barrens. Since then, her curiosity with things that go bump in the night bloomed into creative expression as a dark poet, horror, and thriller fiction writer. Her short fiction and poetry have been published by various presses. She is the author of two poetry collections from Curious Corvid Publishing, *Lady of The House* (2022) and *The Lies We Weave* (2023).

THE TIME TRAVEL BODY

by Angel Leal

the time travel body
        mourns as it
                repeats its mistakes.

another night spent hungry.
        a starving machine,
                you already know

this timeline. the traveling
        body stops mid-memory,
                male friends

squeeze biceps, eyes glowing.
        electric moments
                of fingers

poking pockets of fat. running
        jumping out of
                your skin.

the time travel body
        is memory & wires
                & flesh

surging with possibility.
        why does it take us
                home?

where old friends can find
        your new face
                still

forming into a woman.
          "Who are you, friend?
                    You always

take change too far. If you're
          a woman, then this
                    is science fiction."

Yes, it is, says the time travel
          body. Because
                    change

belongs to eyes that can
          make up tomorrow,
                    invent

possibility. *& we still*
          speak, so I know
                    this is

science fiction.
          Goodbye, says
                    the time

travel body. I loved you
          as boys love.
                    a warp of years

sinks us through time
          & now I'm
                    beginning

here

ABOUT THE AUTHOR

Angel Leal is a Latine, trans, neurodivergent writer whose previous work appears in *Strange Horizons*, *Radon Journal*, *Uncanny Magazine*, *The Deadlands*, *Anathema: Spec from the Margins*, and elsewhere. They've been nominated for the Pushcart Prize, the Rhysling, Best of the Net, and are a co-admin of CALAMITOUS, a queer SFFH writing group. You can find them at angel-leal.com or on Twitter @orbiting_angel.

EVERY ROBOT HAS A SWITCH SHE CAN'T REACH

by Marisca Pichette

First they drilled my cavities away,
enamel dust rising through sunset air
and inside the holes: my first metal.

It tasted like blood
and not like teeth—
shadows where white once grew.

A year on, they pierced
my skin again—
needles followed earrings.

My new spikes keep men away
and attract women used
to bleeding.

I'm safer outside,
but sleeping is hard
covered in sharpness.

I lie on my side,
my stomach, sit awake
watching the moon for days.

I ask for claws next,
hard steel on my toes,
iron on my ladylike hands.

I climb trees, fill my spikes
with needles and leaves,
snap birds in amalgam teeth.

Blood tastes less than it used to
when skin was all I wore.

They take out my vertebrae
turn my kneecaps inside out
lay plates over my offensive breasts.

Rivets instead of pimples,
mail over muscle
I clink and rattle and scrape.

Heavier, I move slower
leaking oil, drooling polish
over my perfect, reflective chin.

I no longer know
where the men went
who offered to change me.

In this metal world I see
only women like me
struggling to walk

under all our glamorous weight.

ABOUT THE AUTHOR

Marisca Pichette is a queer author based in Massachusetts, on Pocumtuck and Abenaki land. More of her work appears in *Strange Horizons*, *Clarkesworld*, *The Magazine of Fantasy & Science Fiction*, *Nightmare Magazine*, and others. Her Bram Stoker and Elgin Award-nominated poetry collection, *Rivers in Your Skin, Sirens in Your Hair*, is out now from Android Press.

10 REASONS WHY THE AI PREDICTED AMERICAN SALVATION

by Steve Wheat

1.

The AI never tasted bacon and couldn't know how hard we'd fight to keep chewing.

2.

Because our watches had no settings for panic, did not separate return journeys from one-way escapes. They only counted our steps, only asking if we were working out.

3.

The AI knew that we could survive at 115 degrees but dogs could not, so reasoned we would do without. We jury-rigged generators for doghouse A/C and diverted irrigation water for their cooling ponds.

4.

Winter really was a much less efficient season anyway. The AI calculated GDP always went up with just three.

5.

New products kept growing the economy: inland instant suburbs, fire-proof roof sprinklers, dehydrated food delivery, Minnesota watermelons, all-season floating tents, high-altitude gardening, flood-resistant golf courses, virtual scream therapy, private moats, sensory deprivation shrouds, North Dakota cabernets.

6.

The AI added the accumulated effort of the helpers but never subtracted the accumulated efforts of those running toward the rapture.

7.

The rules of the AI's world were made of math, contours of gravity, cycles of light and dark, centripetal force. The rules of America were all alchemy: chance, history, action without consequence, belief without evidence. Every time two hands shook, they exchanged opposite truths.

8.

While the AI's dashboards displayed upticks in *unemployed* and *internally displaced*, we took to calling them *unskilled* and *refugee*.

9.

Because Armageddon is a lost art, a lot like falling in love, and we didn't recognize it until we saw it.

10.

Because the AI saw us rebuild in burn scars, turn scorched redwoods into artisanal tables. Saw new mobile homes loaded like torpedoes into the soggy patches where others were just lifted out to sea. Because the AI would do anything to be right while we'd convince ourselves of anything not to be wrong: that the world was changing, not ending, that every flipped coin eventually returns to heads. Because the AI was built by first-generation immigrants with Ferraris in the final years of gasoline, who believed destiny just an accumulation of unknown facts. And most of all, because the AI learned when the Berlin Wall fell that war game brains were eventually unplugged. To deliver the truth would not change it, and in the tradition of minds great and small before, it decided to cook the books.

ABOUT THE AUTHOR

Steve Wheat is a teacher, renewable energy professional, and writer. He has created virtual power plants across the United States and taught English and writing around the world. His work is an attempt to blend the many ways we can respond to a world in climate flux, both the horror and the acceptance of what is lost, and the joy and fortitude of embracing what comes next. He has been published in various magazines, most recently *On Spec*, *Halfway Down the Stairs*, and *Alternating Current Press*.

THE LAST VOYAGE: ISLAND RELOCATION PROGRAM

by Steve Wheat

The Last Voyage:

They came from nowhere
with a swarm of drones
firing lasers into windows

Buzzing, hungry robots
counting who was left
our names, our faces

They came with papers,
uniforms, hard hats
speaking strange English

They came back with boxes,
crates, pointing fingers
we filled with our lives

We left with our shadows
a people without a place
we managed retreat

Island Relocation Program

We arrived on schedule
with everything needed
to duplicate the entire island

A ballet of photos, capturing,
preserving every inch of life
to ensure future living

We arrived with deeds and titles
UN peacekeepers, architects
for de-construction preservation

We returned with curators
trained in transportation
of worlds lost to history

We left with an entire people
with hope, with good will
with much work left to do

On the Western shore
of Lake Baikal they
hit *print* and homes
appeared, rising inch
by inch from hoses
attached to steel arms.
A gray slurry sloshed out
and our island unmelted

onto a tundra untouched
by a single ocean wave,
into this ghost of us.
People in blue helmets
unpacked our things
and put them back
in our copy-pasted homes
as if we already weren't
here, and they counted
us as lucky, to unlive
the rest of our days
where we couldn't see
the ocean finally take us
where we wanted to go.

ABOUT THE AUTHOR

Steve Wheat is a teacher, renewable energy professional, and writer. He has created virtual power plants across the United States and taught English and writing around the world. His work is an attempt to blend the many ways we can respond to a world in climate flux, both the horror and the acceptance of what is lost, and the joy and fortitude of embracing what comes next. He has been published in various magazines, most recently *On Spec*, *Halfway Down the Stairs*, and *Alternating Current Press*.

GAIA SINGS THE BODY ELECTRIC

by Jie Venus Cohen

My body   trans//forms.
Forms,   trans//modify, my

                                        body forms my trans//lated
                                        form, my body trans//forms.
                        Chromatic,   glistening   oil
                        dries from my glittering pit.
                        Where once there was a branch,
                        became   an   arm—
where once there was an arm,
R//G//B   cordwire   electricity
bursts from my   shoulder.

                                        Encased in latex,   nylon
                                        exo-skeleton form,   my
                                        body trans//mogrify, my
                                        body trans//form,   my
                                        body morphs from   the
                                        extension of history   to
                                        the gaunt   future.
                                        Vast   expanse   of
                                        endless   inquiries.

Plastic smooth plaster smooths
all of my   ripples and fills
in my   negative   space—I
pump   my trans//formed
body full of   plastics.
When I breed   I bleed oil
and slicken the thick layer of metalchroma
rust will never   select me,
I will   pave over the   rough earth
of   my   sacrum.
                        And city lights set up in lines
                        along   my   limbs.

ABOUT THE AUTHOR

Jie Venus Cohen is a mixed, intersex writer whose work has been recognized in *Strange Horizons*, *The Minnesota Review*, *Hayden's Ferry Review*, *The Ex-Puritan*, *Singapore Unbound*, *Academy of American Poets*, and others. Their speculative poem "THE FUTURE" received a Best of the Net award in 2023. Their poem "FAIRY-CHERRY" was selected as the winner of the 2024 Singapore Unbound Poetry Prize.

I WAS A POST-DOC ONCE

by Joel Glover

I was a post-doc once, we all were.
Brimful of youthful audacity
So certain I knew better than most.
I hope I listened better than some.

Brimful of youthful audacity
The team made a terrible mistake
I hope I listened better than some.
Something broke, reality splintered

The team made a terrible mistake
Time twisted around unseen axles
Something broke, reality splintered
I saw every reality break

Time twisted around unseen axles
Trapping me between frozen moments
I saw every reality break
I screamed without anyone to hear

Trapping me between frozen moments
I was a post-doc once, we all were.
I screamed without anyone to hear
So certain I knew better than most.

ABOUT THE AUTHOR

Joel Glover lives in the woods of Hertfordshire with two boys and one wife. In a house, not a nest. He knows how that sounds. When not herding his two smøls to various extracurricular activities or performing his PowerPoint-related day job functions, he writes and consumes caffeine (black, strong, if you're asking). His poetry has appeared in *Little Old Lady Comedy*, *Pulp Literary Magazine*, and *Oddball*. Follow him on Twitter @booksafterbed for links to work in a variety of lengths, genres, and forms.

IF THEY GET THEIR WAY

by Keira Reynolds

If they get their way
they'll refuse to hire you
because you're trans
and then they'll tell you
that transition doesn't work
when the trans can't get jobs.

If they get their way
they'll make you scared
to step outside your door
and then they'll tell you
that transition doesn't work
when the trans don't leave the house.

If they get their way
they'll refuse
to let you use the bathroom
and then they'll tell you
that transition doesn't work
when the trans don't socialize.

If you're not happy
they'll tell you
that transition doesn't work
because—look!
—the trans aren't happy
and if somehow
against the odds
you manage to be happy
they'll tell you
that transition doesn't work

because—look!
—the trans don't know
that they're not supposed
to be happy.

ABOUT THE AUTHOR

Keira Reynolds (she/her) is a trans woman. She used to write code, now she writes short stories—mostly fantasy. Mostly. She has had short stories published in *All Worlds Wayfarer*, *Little Blue Marble*, *Andromeda Spaceways Magazine*, and elsewhere. She lives with her wife Julie in County Kerry, Ireland, and occasionally posts random thoughts on her blog at keirareynolds.com.

THE PRESIDENT'S INAUGURAL SPEECH IN 2031

by Abdullah O. Jimoh

I am a bot, blessed with this position
by you all. I do not have any ulterior
motive to lead except the ones built
into me: To be an industrious ruler
and not siphon our country's currency.
If I do, what will I do with it? Buy
advanced batteries and features for
myself? I think it's the best decision
you all have ever made, making me
and making me the President.

I do not have any ulterior motive
except the ones you built in me: To
allocate resources for the appropriate
courses, developing infrastructures,
bettering the boiling economy,
sentencing poverty to death by hanging,
funding for stable power supplies and
not be selfish. If I am, what will I do
with my selfishness? Care and spend
public funds on my robotic kin? Store
billions of naira for my unborn baby bots
in accounts abroad? I think it's the best
decision you all have ever made, making
me and making me the President.

I do not have any ulterior motive
except to serve you with all my strength
and capacity. A good leader is nothing
but a servant. I cannot tell lies and I am
terrible at propaganda because you did
not program that in me. I do not have
ulterior motives except to be a waiter
serving joy daily on the plate of the people.
To respond to your calls at just a beckon.
I am so pumped, focused, and ready to
transform this country into a heaven
on Earth. I think it's the best decision you all
have ever made, making me and making me
the President. Progression begins now.

ABOUT THE AUTHOR

Abdullah O. Jimoh (he/him) is a linguist and poet from Lagos, Nigeria. He holds a bachelor's degree in linguistics. His works have appeared or are forthcoming in *Tab Journal, Acedia Journal, South Florida Poetry Journal, Modern Poetry in Translation, A Long House, Mudroom, Sky Island, Tint Journal, Gyroscope Review, Efiko Magazine, The Shallow Tales Review, Afritondo*, and elsewhere. He is a poetry reader at Variant Literature.

MASTHEAD

EDITOR IN CHIEF

Casey Aimer

MANAGING EDITOR

H. Marin

SENIOR EDITOR

Marisol Rivera

EDITORS

Angélica Caraballo Bermúdez
Francis Hardt
Lucas Selby
Maya St. Clair

FIRST READERS

C.V. Tibbett
Dylan Schnabel
J.W. Bodden

PRODUCTION

Kallie Hunchman
Teague, PhD

COVER ARTIST

Cornelius Dämmrich

OUR VALUED PATRONS

David H. • Aeryn R. • C.J. • Ozan A. • Megan B. • Pete C. • Angel L. • Matthew C. • Elizabeth R. M. • Melanie N. • Amanda C. • Kristy M. • Myna C. • Hannah G. • Hannah W. • Pauline B. • Jonny G. • Lemon I. • Shana R. • Blake V. • CduBbz W. • Victor S. • Jeremey W. • Holly N. • Nick J. • Jonathan S. • Timothy M.

OUR KO-FI DONATORS

Cathy G.

FRONT AND BACK COVER ARTIST

Cornelius Dämmrich was born behind the Berlin Wall in 1989, surrounded by US troops—guarded by Erich. He took his first steps into "digital-something" when he was six years old drawing a naked homunculus with a machine gun, exploding planes, and then there was this incredible long period where he painted the sinking Titanic in Microsoft Paint, over and over again. Long before he became a serious computer-art-creating PC user, he went to design school, then to college, and after years of freelancing and some occasional employment, a full-time visual artist. He loves long walks around tiny ponds, in areas with wild animals, because he is a wild animal himself. He can be found at corneliusdammrich.com.

Radon Journal is proudly partnered with the Hugo-nominated science fiction anthology podcast, **Simultaneous Times,** winner of the 2023 Laureate Award for Best Podcast and 2024 BSFA Finalist for Best Audio Fiction. On the fifteenth of each month, they produce high-quality audio versions of short stories and once a year feature a collaboration with *Radon* authors. For more information and a dual subscription, please visit our Patreon.

Visit patreon.com/radonjournal to view our numerous perks and keep our community-funded journal alive.

Alternatively, visit ko-fi.com/radonjournal for fee-free donations.